Shattered

Shattered

FAMILY FRIENDLY FICTION

LILLIAN KAY DUNCAN

Pleasant Word
A Division of WINEPRESS PUBLISHING

© 2004 by Lillian K. Duncan. All rights reserved.

Printed in the United States of America

Packaged by Pleasant Word, a division of WinePress Publishing, PO Box 428, Enumclaw, WA 98022. The views expressed or implied in this work do not necessarily reflect those of Pleasant Word, a division of WinePress Publishing. Ultimate design, content, and editorial accuracy of this work are the responsibilities of the author.

No part of this publication may be reproduced, stored in a retrieval system, or transmitted in any way by any means—electronic, mechanical, photocopy, recording, or otherwise—without the prior permission of the copyright holder, except as provided by USA copyright law.

Unless otherwise noted, all Scriptures are taken from the Holy Bible, New International Version, Copyright © 1973, 1978, 1984 by the International Bible Society. Used by permission of Zondervan Publishing House. The "NIV" and "New International Version" trademarks are registered in the United States Patent and Trademark Office by International Bible Society.

Scripture references marked KJV are taken from the King James Version of the Bible.

Scripture references marked NASB are taken from the New American Standard Bible, © 1960, 1963, 1968, 1971, 1972, 1973, 1975, 1977 by The Lockman Foundation. Used by permission.

ISBN 1-4141-0125-2
Library of Congress Catalog Card Number: 2004100813

Dedication

This and all that I do is for
God's Glory.

This book is lovingly dedicated
to my husband, Ronny.
You make each day special.

Table of Contents

Acknowledgments 9

Chapter One 11
Chapter Two 23
Chapter Three 33
Chapter Four 55
Chapter Five 67
Chapter Six 85
Chapter Seven 97
Chapter Eight 109
Chapter Nine 117
Chapter Ten 121
Chapter Eleven 123
Chapter Twelve 129
Chapter Thirteen 139
Chapter Fourteen 149
Chapter Fifteen 169

Chapter Sixteen 179
Chapter Seventeen 195
Chapter Eighteen 197
Chapter Nineteen 205
Chapter Twenty 221
Chapter Twenty-one 231
Chapter Twenty-two 239
Chapter Twenty-three 247
Chapter Twenty-four.. 253
Chapter Twenty-five... 259

Acknowledgments

It has been said that no man is an island and that certainly is no less true for writers. A writer would have no story if it weren't for the people and experiences in their life. It would take more space than I have here to express my gratitude to each person that has contributed to my story but here are a few.

A special thanks to Sarah Ban Breathnach and her book, *Simple Abundance.* Had I not read her wonderful book, I am sure that I would never have started writing even though the dream to be a writer has been with me from the beginning.

There aren't enough words to thank my husband, Ronny. Without the loving patience, encouragement, and unending support of Ronny, this book would not have been written nor published. If your picture isn't beside the definition of a ***good husband*** in the dictionary, it should be. It is with deep love that I thank you for all that you have done to assist me in following my dreams.

My family has been enthusiastic supporters of my writing and have never failed to encourage me just when I needed it most. Thanks to my Mom, Herb, Blanche, Barb and their families, Carol, Jay, Eric, Brian, Wendi, Chad, Elizabeth, Brent, Michelle, Jeremy, Brad, and Jeremy. I think we are so lucky that we all like each other as much as we love each other. I certainly don't want to forget my wonderful in-laws, who are too numerous to mention by name but certainly are no less important in my life. I love you all.

I would be remiss if I didn't mention my book club buddies from so long ago (well, not that long ago.) You were my first readers and critics and your gentleness was appreciated. Thanks to Mary Krnich, Mary Warshaw, Natalie Spagnola, Judi Gee and last but certainly not least Kathryn Rieter for their encouragement.

And to Annie Dargols, life may have moved us in different directions and to different parts of the country but that only makes our friendship more precious. Your courage to face each day and make the most of the life that God gives is truly amazing. I am a better person for having known you.

There are so many other people that could and should be included but aren't. Please forgive me for any lapses.

Peace and love to all of you.

Chapter One

It was Monday morning and so Jenni was cleaning the house. She wrinkled her nose at the pungent smell of the lemon cleaner. Jenni plugged in the vacuum and soon was absorbed in the mindless back and forth motion, debating the pros and cons of upcoming vacation choices.

She was pushing for a cultural expedition through Europe, but Michael wanted something more adventuresome. It wasn't that she wouldn't enjoy that type of a vacation, but it seemed as if her dream of a tour of European art museums might never happen if she didn't put her foot down and insist upon it.

She smiled. She wasn't very good at putting her foot down, at least not to Michael. She loved him so much that it was hard to say no to him. It didn't really bother her since he was the same way with her. She knew they would end up in some rainforest or on a mountain somewhere battling bugs, but it never hurt to make her hus-

Shattered

band work a little bit for what he wanted. She didn't want him to take her for granted too much.

There was no sense of doom as she heard the ringing of the phone over the noise of the vacuum and frowned. For a brief second, she thought of letting the machine pick up, but her curiosity got the best of her. She didn't know why she even bothered keeping the answering machine plugged in since she rarely used it.

She walked to the phone, not knowing that her life was about to change. All she felt was annoyance at the interruption. But the annoyance quickly turned to concern when she heard her husband's voice.

Michael's voice was shaky and slurred, and she had difficulty understanding his words. "Jenni, I've been arrested."

Her heart stopped. She shook her head and told herself to breathe. She must have misunderstood, but he repeated the same message and added, "I'm in jail, call Robbie." Then, he hung up before she could tell him that she loved him.

She hit the familiar numbers with shaky fingers. Roberto was Michael's best friend as well as their attorney. Roberto was stunned, but he assured her in a calm voice that he would take care of the misunderstanding, whatever it was.

Ten minutes later, Jenni was sprinting up the steps of the police station, only to find Roberto blocking her way. His face was pale. He took hold of her arm, but

Chapter One

she pulled away and tried to push past him. She didn't have time to waste. She needed to get to Michael. She needed to see him. He needed her. But then she saw the expression on Roberto's face and she stopped. This time she felt the sense of doom.

"What's wrong?" she asked, trying to keep the fear out of her voice but failing.

"Michael's been taken to the hospital. I'll drive."

"The hospital?" She was confused, but when she saw the look on Roberto's face, she didn't ask for an explanation but instead grabbed his hand, and they hurried to his car.

Once they were in the car, Jenni turned to Roberto. She said, "What is going on? What's wrong with Michael?"

Roberto shook his head. "I'm not sure. When I got there, they told me that Michael had collapsed and was on the way to the hospital."

"Why was he arrested? I don't understand any of this."

"He's been charged with embezzling, but that's all I know for now. I'll get more information later."

"*Embezzlement,*" Jenni repeated back in a shocked voice. She'd assumed that he'd had some sort of accident that was his fault. It hadn't even occurred to her that it was a criminal matter. "Embezzling. Michael won't even take the wrong change at a store. He would never steal money. That's just crazy."

Roberto glanced at her. "I know, but I didn't have time to get details. I'll deal with it later."

Shattered

Jenni's heart was pounding so loudly it was hard for her to focus on Roberto's words. Her mind was racing. Nothing felt real. Everything was happening so fast, and she didn't understand any of it. "Why did Michael collapse? Was it a heart attack?"

Roberto just shook his head. He didn't have any answers. They pulled into the hospital parking lot. The car hadn't come to a complete stop when Jenni jumped out and dashed toward the emergency room doors. Roberto was right behind her. He hadn't bothered to park. At the moment, he didn't care how many tickets they gave him for parking in the wrong space.

Jenni raced to the information desk at the emergency room. "My husband is Michael Hamilton. He was just brought in here. I want to see him."

The nurse looked up with annoyance on her face. "Ma'am, you will have to wait your turn. I'm busy with someone else now." She pointed at a young woman slouched in the chair holding her side.

"No, I want to know where my husband is." She had to find Michael. She needed to see him with her own eyes. Roberto touched her elbow. She looked up at him.

"Let's go. We'll find him ourselves."

Jenni turned to leave with Roberto. They walked toward a door that led to the emergency room. The nurse jumped up out of her seat forgetting about the sick woman sitting in the chair. She jumped in front of them blocking the entrance with her body.

Chapter One

"You aren't going anywhere. I don't know who you think you are, but—"

Roberto's dark eyes flashed, but he spoke calmly. "Then, perhaps you will be kind enough to help us find Michael Hamilton and see what is happening with him."

The nurse sighed. "Hold on." She marched off through the door that she had been blocking. Roberto paced while they waited for her to come back. It seemed an eternity, but she finally came back. She looked at Roberto. "Is that the man that came in with the police?" She asked it loudly enough to make heads turn toward them.

He nodded.

"He's with the doctors. That's all I know." She nodded at Jenni. "Is that his wife?"

"Yes."

The nurse stepped toward Roberto and leaned in. She whispered to him, "It doesn't look good. They're trying to revive him."

Jenni interrupted. "What are you saying? He's my husband. I have a right to know."

The nurse patted Jenni's shoulder. "They're doing their best, hon. Just sit over there, and I'll go back in a few minutes and check on him for you again."

Jenni tolerated the patting and nodded. She went over and sat in an ugly green plastic chair. The TV blared with cartoons even though no one was watching. Most eyes were on Jenni but she didn't notice. She spent the next several minutes alternating between sitting down, then standing up, then pacing some more, and then she finally threw herself in the chair. She lowered her head and began praying. There wasn't anything else she could do at the moment.

The nurse walked the young woman back through the door that she'd blocked Jenni and Roberto from going in. In a few minutes she returned and approached Jenni and Roberto. They both looked up at her. She gave a small shrug.

"Sorry, you can't go back yet. Someone will be here soon."

"How is he?" Jenni asked.

The nurse shook her head and answered more kindly, "I don't have any information yet. Sorry."

Jenni nodded and tried to smile. She sat there twisting her wedding ring. She took it off and ran her finger along the letters that had been engraved inside, "gmfl."

The letters were a promise from Michael. He wouldn't die. He couldn't die. He was her whole life. She didn't have a life if he wasn't in it. She felt the raised letters again. He'd promised her that they would be together forever. He couldn't die.

Jenni resumed her routine of sitting, standing, and walking the length of the waiting room and continuously praying as she did. Roberto sat patiently in his chair watching Jenni but knowing there was no reason to try and calm her down.

Chapter One

He was accustomed to waiting, but he knew it was hard for most people. He'd waited for deliberating juries to come to a decision for more hours than he could count. He tried to comfort Jenni, but she was having no part of it. She kept moving and glaring at the nurse at the desk.

After ten minutes, she threw herself back into the chair. She doubled over and put her head in her hands. She looked at Roberto through her fingers. Her voice quivered. "This is a nightmare. I just don't understand."

He patted her shoulder. "I know, I know. None of it makes any sense, but we'll take care of it later. Do you want me to call Carmen or maybe your mom?"

She looked at him. His own dark eyes reflected the worry she felt. She shook her head. There was no sense getting other people upset. They didn't know anything yet. She jumped back up and headed for the nurse's station yet again determined to find out what was happening. The nurse ignored her for several moments and then looked calmly up at Jenni as if she'd never seen her before in her life.

"Yes?"

"I need to know what's happening with my husband. I don't even know what's wrong with him. Why was he brought in?" Her voice faltered and the tears threatened to come. She took a deep breath.

The nurse relented. She sighed and stood up. "I'll go check. Hold on a minute."

Shattered

When she came back, she smiled kindly at Jenni for the first time. She spoke softly. "Let's go over here and talk." Together they walked back to Roberto.

Jenni slumped back into her seat.

"What's going on?" Jenni asked. She'd meant it to come out sounding firm and in control, but instead her voice was panicked.

The nurse smiled at her and spoke gently. "He's in cardiac arrest, and the doctors are trying to stabilize him. I'm sorry, there's not much more I can tell you right now."

"Can I see him?"

"Sorry, not right now, but a doctor will be out just as soon as possible." She patted Jenni's shoulder. "The doctor is very good. Your husband is in good hands."

"Thanks," Jenni mumbled and sat down. She turned to Roberto. "Cardiac arrest? How can that be? He just had a check up a few weeks ago and everything was fine."

Before Roberto could answer, the door to the emergency room opened; Jenni looked up and saw Nicholas Peyton marching toward them. Nicholas was the owner of the company that Michael was being accused of stealing money from.

"Jenni, dear, I just heard about Mic—"

Before he could finish, Jenni jumped up. Roberto put a hand on her to stop her, but she threw it off without a glance and walked over to Nicholas Peyton.

Her voice became more shrill with each word. "What did you do to Michael? Why did you have him

Chapter One

arrested? He would never steal from you. You know that. What is going—"

Nicholas stepped back from Jenni. He had the look of a deer caught in headlights at night. "Jenni, dear, I can't discuss any of that. But when I heard that Michael had collapsed, I came right over. I'm just as worri—"

She turned to Roberto and demanded of him, "You ask him. You find out what is going on. Why is he saying Michael stole from him?"

Roberto put a calming hand on Jenni's arm. He whispered, "Jenni, this isn't the place or the time. We'll get everything sorted out later, but right now let's just stay calm and—"

She whirled away from both men and resumed her pacing. The men watched her for a moment. Then Roberto turned back to Nicholas Peyton.

"I think you should leave, Nicholas. I know you meant well, but your being here is upsetting Jenni. I'll call you later when I find out how Michael is doing."

"I didn't mean to upset her. I was just worried . . . I didn't mean for this to happen. I had to protect my company."

Roberto didn't respond to Nicholas Peyton's words. "We shouldn't be talking to each other at this point. I'll call you later."

He watched Nicholas leave before he turned back to Jenni. She was slumped in the chair. He walked over and touched her shoulder. "Don't worry about Nicholas. Let's focus on Michael." He hesitated for a moment and then asked gently, "Maybe I should call your mom and let her know what's going on?"

"No." Her head jerked up at his suggestion understanding what he meant. He thought her mother should be here in case something bad happened to Michael. It wouldn't, *couldn't* happen to Michael. He was her whole life.

"No," she repeated more calmly. "He's going to be fine. He's going to be fine."

He had to be fine. Bad things like this weren't supposed to happen to good people like Michael. She felt the first tear slip out. She took several deep breaths. She wouldn't let herself fall apart. Michael needed her, and she would be here for him just the way he'd always been there for her.

Jenni was sitting next to Roberto when she saw the woman walk through the double doors of the emergency room. The woman was dressed in green scrubs, and her mouth was grim. Jenni noticed the woman's eyes. They were sad. The woman walked up to the nurse. The two of them conferred for a moment and both turned and looked at Jenni.

That was the moment Jenni knew.

Jenni lost all sense of reality. The woman walked in slow motion toward Jenni, as if walking through Jell-O. Roberto took hold of Jenni's hand and his

Chapter One

mouth moved, but Jenni couldn't hear his words. The doctor began to speak.

Chapter Two

It was two months later and Jenni lay in bed. She hadn't been out of the house since the day of Michael's funeral. She had stopped talking to anyone other than her mother and even that was as little as possible.

She lay in her bed trying to forget the things she'd been told and yet was able to think of nothing else. She didn't know the man they talked about, but it certainly wasn't her beloved husband. Her husband had been a good man, an honorable man who could be trusted. She didn't know how to live without Michael by her side.

The police had taken her husband away from her. They had told her that their love, their marriage, their life together had been an illusion. It wasn't enough that her husband was dead, but they'd taken everything away from her that day, her love, her marriage and, her identity.

Shattered

The first few days after the funeral she'd gone through the motions. Getting up, putting on clothes, eating breakfast, sitting in a chair, then moving to a different chair, eating lunch, then sitting again until dinner, and then finally back to her own empty bed.

Then, it had occurred to her that she didn't have to pretend that she was all right. Michael wasn't there for her to take care of. Michael wasn't there for him to be disappointed by her behavior, so she went to bed.

The minutes turned into hours. The hours turned into days and then weeks. When people came into the room to talk with her, she would turn away, refusing their comfort. She could hear the worried voices swirling around her. She didn't want their comfort. She didn't want anything from anyone. They eventually stopped coming and that was fine with her. If she couldn't trust Michael, she couldn't trust anyone.

It wasn't just that her husband had died, but the foundation of her life had collapsed. If Michael were an illusion then that meant it had all been an illusion. Their life together hadn't been real, nor was their love, and if that wasn't real, then her whole life had been an illusion.

Her life had happily revolved around her husband, and now he was gone. She'd been proud to be Michael's wife and to take care of him, but now it had all been taken away from her with a few simple words. The police had taken it all away from her with their ugly accusations. She hadn't just lost her husband, but she'd lost everything, including a reason to get out of bed.

Chapter Two

There was a knock on her door, no doubt her mother. She turned her back to the door and squeezed her eyes shut. She heard the door open.

"Jenni," she heard her mother calling softly, "you've got company, dear."

"No, I don't want to see anyone. Maybe later."

The door closed. She let out her breath. Good. She was alone again.

"Hi, Jenni."

She jumped at the sound of a voice but didn't open her eyes or turn around. She willed the voice to go away.

"You might as well turn over and look at me. I'm not leaving until we talk." He spoke softly, but she could hear the steely determination in his voice.

"I don't want to talk to you. I don't feel good. Maybe later."

"That's fine. I'll sit here until you do feel better." She heard the soft scraping of the chair moving against the carpet.

"Leave me alone."

"No."

"Go away."

"No."

"I don't want to talk to you."

The man could hear a hint of anger in her words. He smiled. That was good. He wanted her to feel something other than self-pity.

"I want to talk to you."

25

Shattered

"No, go away. I don't want you here. I don't want to talk to you. I don't want you to talk to me. I just want to be left alone. I have earned the right to be left alone, Sam. Go away."

She sat up cross-legged in the bed and yelled at the man. "You have no idea what it's like. I don't want to hear your lies about how it will be OK. How God will take care of me! It's not true. He didn't take care of Michael. Michael's dead. God let Michael die."

At the sound of her words, she moaned and slumped back to the bed. "Michael's dead." She said it again through her sobbing. Sam moved to the bed and rubbed her back as she cried. After her sobbing subsided, she lifted her head. Sam handed her a tissue box. She blew her nose loudly and let out several deep breaths, then looked at the man sitting on the side of her bed.

"What are you doing here?" she asked him.

"Carmen called me and told me that you haven't been out of the house since the funeral and now you are refusing to talk to people. I was in the States and decided to stop here before I go back to Bolivia. Michael wouldn't be happy about the way you are acting."

At the mention of Michael's name, something snapped. She yelled, "I don't care whether Michael would be happy or not. Look what he did to me. He didn't care about me. It was all lies. He never loved me."

She flopped back down on the bed and began to cry again. Sam sat patiently waiting for her to stop.

Chapter Two

After several minutes, she did. She sat back up and looked at Sam.

Sam had been the man that led both Michael and her to Christ. He'd changed their lives but now it didn't matter. Jenni knew it had all been lies. Her faith had been real but apparently even that had been more lies from Michael. His faith had not been real or he would never have done the things he'd been accused of.

She sighed. None of it mattered now. She'd done what she was supposed to do, and Jesus hadn't kept his part of the bargain.

Sam had been a minister and their next door neighbor years ago. Now, he was a missionary in Bolivia, and he looked the part. His graying hair was shaggy, and it looked as if he were trying to grow a beard.

"You look a mess," she said.

"So do you," he told her right back.

They stared at each other for a moment and then both laughed.

"How's Barbara?"

"She's fine. We're both very worried about you."

"I'm fine."

"If you're fine, what are you doing in bed, then?"

She shrugged. "Why not? It's not like I have anything else to do."

"I'll tell you why not. You didn't die. You have to get up and start living again. I can't imagine the pain you're living with, but you are living. You can't just stay in bed forever."

Shattered

She shrugged again. "I might."

He picked up her hand. "Jenni, I know this is all so horrible, and I'm not going to pretend it's not, but you've got to start living again. God will help you through this if you just let him."

She pulled back her hand. "No. This is God's fault. He let all this happen."

"Jenni, you can't let this rob you of your faith."

"It already has." She spoke quietly and the tears started again.

"I don't believe that." He stood up and stretched. He sat back down. "Let God help you. He's right here. All you have to do is reach out to him. I can't explain why tragedies happen to people, but I know that God will help you through this if you let him."

Jenni didn't speak but she nodded.

Sam looked at Jenny with his earnest blue eyes. "Barbara and I have talked about this many times. We don't believe Michael did any of the things they said."

"You don't?" she asked.

"You do?" he asked her back.

Her eyes filled with tears. "Do I have a choice?"

He patted her hand. "We always have a choice, Jenni."

She said nothing for a few moments. "You really don't believe the police?"

"No, of course not. Michael was an honest man. He wouldn't have ever done those things."

"But they said—"

Chapter Two

"I don't care what they say, they are mistaken. I refuse to let them steal the good memories of Michael that I have. I am very sad that he died, but I knew Michael very well, and I don't believe the accusations. I also know that Michael is in a much better place now."

She said nothing. Her head hung down and she wiped away the tears. *How could she have so easily believed the lies about Michael? Why had she been so willing to believe the ugly accusations?* She worked to regain her composure. When she had, she looked back up at Sam. She smiled.

"I can't stay long. I only have a few hours here before my plane leaves. Will you pray with me?"

She nodded. After Sam prayed, they talked about some of the good memories of Michael, and then he hugged her and he was gone. She lay back on the bed, trying to recapture her self-pity but couldn't. It was gone.

She slowly sat up and swung her legs off the bed. She stood up on shaky legs and walked to the bathroom. She caught a glimpse of herself in the mirror and was shocked. She did look awful. Sam hadn't been lying about that.

Her hair hung in clumps around her shoulder. She couldn't remember the last time that she'd shampooed or even combed it. Dark circles outlined her eyes. Her skin was pasty and white. She looked horrible.

Shattered

She sank to the floor, sobbing, "Michael, Michael." She rocked back and forth. She curled up on the bathroom floor. She cried and rocked back and forth.

She heard Michael's voice. "Jenni. I love you."

She cried back, "No, no, you didn't love me. You never loved me. If you loved me, you wouldn't have left me alone with all of this."

"Open your eyes, Jenni. I want you to look at me."

"No, you can't make me," she yelled. "I'm mad at you."

"Jenni, I love you. You know I have loved you every day since the day I met you."

She opened her eyes. Michael sat beside her on the bathroom floor. He smiled at her. His arms went around her. She leaned against him feeling his warmth. She felt safe for the first time in months.

She shook her head. "No, you don't love me. They said—"

"I know what they said, Jenni. The question is do you believe them?"

"No, I don't believe you could do those things, but they said—"

He caressed her hair. "Then, don't believe it, Jenni. Know that I love you and I will always love you, but now it's time for you to start living again. We were like the geese, we mated for life but now I'm gone and you're still alive. God still has plans for you and you need to get up and start living those plans."

"No." She shook her head against his chest. "I can't. I don't want to."

Chapter Two

"It's time now. You can't stay in bed forever."

She felt him pull away. "No, don't leave."

"I love you, Jenni."

She felt coldness where his warm chest had been. She opened her eyes. The coldness was the tile floor of her own bathroom. She sat up and leaned against the tub. She felt the wetness on her cheeks. It had only been a dream. Michael hadn't been there, holding her, comforting her. It had only been a dream.

She smiled; but it had been a wonderful dream. She could still feel the warmth of his arms, hear the love in his voice. The love. He had loved her. It didn't matter what anyone told her; she knew that Michael had loved her.

She glanced down at the ring still on her finger. She pulled it off and felt the ridges of the engraved letters, "gmfl." Michael engraved those letters into each piece of jewelry that he gave her. It was his promise to her that he wouldn't ever stop loving her or ever leave her the way her father had.

She smiled. She believed in that promise. She believed in Michael. He hadn't betrayed her or their wedding vows.

She pulled herself up to her knees and, using the tub as an altar, she began to pray. Sam had said God would help; all she had to do was ask. Her prayer was simple. *Please God, help me. I need your strength.* She repeated the words over and over. First the prayer was silent, but then she was saying it aloud.

She took a deep breath.

Please God, help me. I need your strength.

The police were wrong.

Please God, help me. I need your strength.

She felt peace cascading over her.

Please God, help me. I need your strength.

She felt energy bubbling up inside her for the first time in months.

Please God, help me. I need your strength.

She opened her eyes and smiled. God was still there. He'd only been waiting for her to ask for help. Michael had not betrayed her. Michael was not a thief and a criminal. He was an honest man. He was a good man. She knew him better than anyone in the world, and she knew he wouldn't do the horrible things they'd said.

Their life together had been real. Their life together had meant something, and she wouldn't let anyone take that from them. She stood up. She didn't know why they were saying the things they were saying, but they were wrong. The police had made a mistake. A big mistake that had somehow cost Michael his life.

The police were wrong, and she was going to prove it. She might not be able to bring Michael back, but she could restore his name, his dignity, and his honor. She knew the truth. Her husband hadn't done those things, and she wouldn't rest until the world knew it.

Chapter Three

Beth Collins stood at the stove cooking eggs for her daughter, a spatula in one hand and a cigarette in the other. She took a long drag off the cigarette, then flipped the egg. She knew cooking wasn't what Jenni needed, but it was all she had to offer. She didn't know what to do for her daughter, but then again she'd never been able to comfort Jenni.

At least when she cooked Beth felt as if she were doing something useful. Jenni needed more help than Beth could give her, and indeed she had even consulted a psychiatrist a few weeks earlier with the help of Nicholas Peyton and Annie Meyers.

Both of them had every right to turn their backs on Jenni, but they hadn't. Nicholas had been so kind even though it was his company that Michael had stolen from. He'd given Beth the name of a doctor and had even called her for Beth and explained the situation. He'd

Shattered

come over several times and helped Beth with financial things that she just didn't understand.

Annie had been just as helpful through the whole mess. She'd stopped in more than once to check on Jenni and each time that she came she would call beforehand to see what Beth needed in the way of groceries. She always refused the money that Beth would offer her.

The doctor had told Beth to give Jenni more time and prescribed Zoloft, but it didn't seem to be helping. It had been more than a week since Jenni had even come downstairs and more than three weeks since she'd bothered getting dressed.

Maybe Sam's visit would help. He'd told her that he thought he'd gotten through to Jenni. She hoped so.

Beth had survived two divorces and the deaths of two other husbands, so she certainly understood the pain of losing a spouse, but she couldn't begin to imagine the torment Jenni was in. To learn that your husband was dead was horrible enough, but to find out that he had betrayed you as well. Beth wiped tears away with the corner of the dishtowel.

She hated that Jenni was in so much pain, but she didn't know how to help her. Beth had never been able to help Jenni. She'd done the best she could for Jenni as a child, but it hadn't been enough. Jenni had never gotten over her father leaving her, but Michael had given Jenni the security she'd always craved, and then he'd ripped that security from her. He might as well have ripped out her heart.

Chapter Three

Beth heard footsteps and turned to find Jenni standing in the doorway, her brown shoulder-length hair still wet from a shower. Beth quickly stabbed out the cigarette, but Jenni didn't notice it.

"Well, good morning, sweetheart." She made her voice cheerful. "I was just making eggs for your breakfast, but I can make something else. Pancakes, sausage, whatever you want."

"No, the eggs are just fine, Mom."

Beth covertly examined Jenni as they ate in silence. She'd lost weight and there were dark circles under her eyes, but Jenni seemed better. Maybe that medicine the doctor had given was starting to work, or maybe the visit from Sam had helped.

Just the fact that Jenni had come downstairs without any prodding was enough to give Beth a sense of hope that her daughter was returning from the dark place she'd been.

Jenni gave her mother a wan smile. "I'm sorry I've been such a pain, Mom."

"You have been no such thing. You've had the shock of your life. No one expected you to act as if nothing happened. Believe me, I know it's not easy. Of course, I always had you to think of and that helped."

Jenni looked at the eggs and moved them around with her fork. "It's not true."

"What's not true, honey?" Beth sat down by the table with coffee. She drummed her fingers on the table. She wanted a cigarette, but Jenni didn't like people smoking in the house.

"The things they're saying about Michael. He didn't steal that money, and he didn't kill himself."

Her mother wanted to protest, but she knew that tone and knew it would be useless to argue, and, besides, if that's what Jenni needed to believe, that was fine with her. She just wanted her daughter to get better.

Jenni took a bite of egg, then spoke. Her blue eyes glittered with unshed tears. "You've known Michael for almost twenty-five years, Mom. Do you honestly believe he would steal money? He would get mad at me when I didn't give a store clerk back the extra amount when they made a mistake in our favor."

"I know, dear, but—" Beth reached in her pocket for a cigarette but stopped herself.

Jenni stood up and paced. "But nothing. If the police hadn't told you, would you ever believe in a million years that he would do something like that?"

"No, I guess I wouldn't have believed it, but—" Beth conceded the point. Michael's honesty had always been above reproach. He may have been the only person in America that didn't do creative tax reporting.

"But nothing." Jenni sat down on the edge of the kitchen chair. "And now, just because the police say it's true, I'm supposed to believe that my husband was a fraud. I don't think so, and what's more I'm going to prove that they are lying."

Chapter Three

Jenni glared at her mother as if Beth Collins were somehow personally responsible for the accusations. Beth had thought that she was glad of the change in Jenni, but now she wasn't so sure. She didn't like Jenni being so agitated.

Jenni looked up with wild eyes. "Someone murdered him."

"Now, honey. That's ridiculous." Beth reached for the cigarette and this time lit it. Jenni didn't notice.

"No more ridiculous than Michael embezzling money or killing himself, but you just want to believe the bad things they're saying. He didn't do it," Jenni yelled at her mother.

Beth moved to the counter and opened assorted vitamin bottles and added two Zoloft. The doctor had only prescribed one, but Beth was becoming increasingly worried about Jenni. She handed them to Jenni with a glass of milk.

Instead of taking them, Jenni set them on the table distractedly. Jenni continued to explain why the police were wrong. Beth watched as Jenni took each vitamin one at a time, but the Zoloft stayed on the table. Soon, they were the only ones left. Jenni picked up one of the little white pills and looked at them with interest and then at her mother.

"What is this?"

Her mother worked hard not to show the anxiety she was feeling. "The doctor prescribed it for you. She thought it would help."

"What doctor? What is it, Mother?"

"I believe it's Zoloft, honey." She said the words softly, knowing her daughter would be angry.

Jenni continued to examine the pills. "You've been drugging me."

Her mother tried to explain. "It's not like that, Jenni. The doctor felt you needed something to help you out of this depression. It was such a shock when . . . well, you know."

"I'll say I've had a shock. My husband has been murdered and no one seems to care. I can't believe Dr. Joseph would prescribe something without talking with me about it." She continued looking at the pill. She looked up at her mother with hurt gleaming in her blue eyes.

"He didn't, honey. It was another doctor." Her hand jerkily stubbed out the cigarette.

"What doctor? Dr. Joseph is my doctor."

"Mr. Peyton thought maybe you needed some more help, and he—"

Jenni jumped up and then sat back down. "Nicholas Peyton helped kill Michael. I can't believe you think you can trust him. I can't believe you're part of it."

"Part of what, honey?" Panic seeped into Beth Collins's voice.

Jenni stood up, motioning wildly. "Part of this, this whole thing to make me believe these bad things about Michael."

Chapter Three

"I'm not, honey." She spoke softly, hoping to calm Jenni. "The doctor said the pills would make you feel better. That's all. I'm not trying to hurt you."

Jenni threw the pills at her. "Then, why would you give me these?"

Her mother stood up, shocked at Jenni's behavior. "Jennifer, you need to calm down."

"No, what I need to do is prove that my husband wasn't a criminal." Jenni walked to the door, grabbing her keys along the way.

"Where are you going? I don't think you should be driving."

Jenni whirled around. "What? Now, I'm a prisoner in my own home."

Her mother called her name again, but Jenni ignored her and kept walking. The door banged shut, and then the car started up and pulled out of the drive. Beth lit a cigarette and took a deep breath and then walked to the phone.

Once Jenni was in the car, she wasn't sure where to go. She felt disoriented, unsure of herself. She hadn't been out of the house since the day of Michael's funeral. She needed to prove Michael was innocent but didn't know where to begin.

After driving around aimlessly for a half-hour, she drove to the only place that made sense. Roberto was more than their attorney. He'd been Michael's best friend since childhood. He'd help her prove that they were lying about Michael. He would know what to do.

Shattered

Most of that day was fuzzy, but she was sure that Roberto knew much more than he'd told her. She had never talked to the police or any investigators of any type, which seemed odd to her. Roberto must have interceded.

She pulled into the mall and drove around until she found a parking spot. Michael had teased Roberto endlessly about having his office in a mall, but in reality, it had been a great marketing idea. When he'd first opened up, he'd made up a sign that invited shoppers in to ask general legal questions. It had worked like a charm. Shoppers would often stop in to ask a simple question and end up becoming paying clients.

Roberto hadn't wanted to be a corporate lawyer. He'd wanted to help people with their problems, and he was good enough to make a decent living from it. Occasionally, he would do work for The Marshall Corporation to supplement his income. He'd been offered to work exclusively for The Marshall Corporation more than once but he'd refused, citing his autonomy as the reason.

Jenni pulled into a parking space. She walked into Roberto's office.

Roberto's part-time secretary and full-time wife, Carmen, was sitting at the desk talking on the phone when Jenni entered the office. She dropped the phone and rushed to Jenni. Jenni allowed herself to be hugged. Both women's faces were streaked with tears when they separated.

Chapter Three

"Oh, Jenni. I have been so worried. I've called your house and stopped over, but your mother said you weren't up to visitors. I called Sam. I hope you're not mad at me." Carmen had just a hint of a Hispanic accent. Jenni and Carmen had been friends since Carmen had married Roberto more than seventeen years before.

They'd spent countless hours together at cookouts, birthday parties, and family vacations. Michael and Jenni were their regular baby-sitters, except when they were going out with Roberto and Carmen.

"No, I'm not mad. He did help me. I'm feeling better, and it doesn't surprise me that Mom kept you from talking to me. She was giving me drugs without me knowing. Did you know that?" Jenni demanded.

Carmen looked shocked. "No, I didn't. Why would she do that?"

Jenni shrugged. "I don't know. I need to talk to Roberto."

"Of course." Carmen took her hand and led her to the door. She knocked and then opened the door without waiting for a response from her husband. Roberto looked up from the newspaper he was reading. He immediately leapt up out of his seat and went to Jenni. He enclosed her in his burly arms. Jenni resisted for a moment then relaxed.

When they separated, he held her at arms' length. His voice choked with emotion. "Jenni, how are you? We've missed you so much."

Shattered

"I have questions."

Roberto nodded but didn't look happy. He had hoped that Jenni would just put the circumstances of Michael's death out of her mind and go about the business of healing, but he should have known better. Jenni was not one to take the easy way out.

Carmen and Roberto exchanged uneasy glances, and Carmen began to back out of the office. "I'll just let you two alone so you can talk."

Jenni didn't let go of Carmen's hand. "No, Carmen. I want you here. You're my friend. I don't have anything to hide from you."

"I know, but . . ."

Jenni gave her a brave smile. "It's OK. Really, I'm ready to hear it, but I'd like you to be here to hear it with me. I don't really remember much from that day, so you better start at the beginning."

Carmen relented and moved back into the office, still holding Jenni's hand. They sat down at a round conference table in the corner of the office near the window. None of them noticed the brilliant sunshine streaming in through the window.

Roberto looked up at Jenni and smiled. "Are you sure you want to do this, Jen? Why not just put it behind you and move on? I've taken care of everything. There's no reason for you to put yourself through another ordeal."

Jenni's shoulder-length brown hair swished as she shook her head. "Because I don't believe any of it. That's

Chapter Three

why, and I can't believe that you do. He was your friend. You know what kind of a man he is . . . was. He wouldn't do the things they said."

Roberto blinked at the verbal assault but said nothing to defend himself. "I didn't believe it until I saw the evidence." He waited a moment and then met her eyes. "I know it's hard to believe, but I saw papers with his signature on them."

"I don't care what you've seen. I know my husband and I believe in him." Jenni sat ramrod straight in the chair and stared intently at her friends. He knew better than to argue with her.

"Jenni, this is painful for me, too. He was like a brother to me. I don't understand why he would do these things, and I didn't want to believe them, but I've seen enough to know that it looks as if the charges are true. Jenni, go home and come back when you're stronger. Better yet, just go home and forget about all this."

Jenni sat quietly in the chair wondering if she could. Just go home and grieve for her husband. It would be so much easier if she could, but she knew she couldn't. She owed Michael too much to do that. He would never have given up on her, and she wasn't going to give up on him.

She gave Roberto a sad look and shook her head. "They are saying that the Michael that we knew and loved was a lie, and I don't believe that. Do you?"

Their eyes met. He shook his head but didn't say anything.

43

Shattered

He walked over to a file cabinet and pulled out a thick file. He came back over to the table but didn't open the file. He took a deep breath and began. "Michael began making a few small transfers to a company in the Bahamas two years ago. There were invoices showing that The Marshall Corporation was buying materials from it. All the bills had Michael's signature as the approving signature."

He pushed a paper toward her and pointed at the name. "Isn't that his signature?"

Jenni looked and nodded.

"At first, it wasn't big amounts, then it slowly went up to five thousand dollars every month. Then, about a year ago, the amounts became increasingly larger, eventually reaching the three million dollar mark in a very short period of time." He stopped, but she nodded for him to continue.

"With such large expenditures, the auditors investigated further and found no such company existed except on paper. The money had been transferred from the Bahamas account to an offshore account in the Cayman Islands where it became untraceable. The auditors approached Nicholas Peyton. He contacted the police. Their investigation eventually led to Michael's arrest."

He pulled out some papers and handed one to Jenni. She looked at it.

Chapter Three

"This is a copy of an authorization form transferring money to the account with Michael's signature on it." He held up the stack. "These are more of the same."

Jenni looked at the signature at the bottom of the paper. She drew in a quick breath. It was Michael's signature. "Maybe he didn't know what he was signing. Is this all the proof?"

Roberto grimaced. "It doesn't matter, Jen. That should be enough. Just accept it."

She didn't say anything and so Roberto took a deep breath. He cleared his throat nervously. "I don't know what you remember, but Michael bought property in the Bahamas. He bought a restaurant and a house. They were then given as gifts to a Jasmine DuPree. They aren't quite sure where the money came from. It didn't come from Michael's personal accounts or anywhere else they could find."

Jenni flinched as if she'd been hit. She'd known it was coming, but it hurt just the same. She closed her eyes as she felt the pain threatening to rush in, but she refused to allow it. She opened them and gave Carmen a small smile.

Carmen looked incredulous. "What are you saying, Robbie? That Michael bought this house for this woman?" She hadn't known this part of the story.

He nodded slowly. "And it appears as if Michael was getting ready to move to the Bahamas. He had applied

Shattered

for a long-term visa to live there." He handed her another paper. "The police found it in his desk at work."

Carmen protested loudly, her accent thickened. "I don't believe that. Michael would never have left Jenni. Michael wasn't the kind of person to do things like this, and he loved her so much." She pounded the table for emphasis.

Jenni gave her friend a grateful smile. She was glad to know that someone realized how crazy this all was. Roberto held up a hand to calm Carmen. He knew how worked up she could get, and the last thing Jenni needed was to have someone else playing into her denial of reality.

"I know it's hard to believe, honey, but like I said, I've seen the proof. I didn't want to believe it either."

Carmen shook her head vehemently. "This is just ridiculous."

The phone rang, so Roberto walked over to his desk to answer it. He spoke softly as he watched the two women whispering.

"Yes, she is." He was silent as he listened to the other person.

"No, she seems fine, just determined not to believe it, but I think that's to be expected under the circumstances. At least she's up and out of bed. That's an improvement." He nodded as he listened and glanced nervously back at the two women. They weren't paying attention to him.

Chapter Three

He whispered into the phone, "Yes, I will see to that."

He walked back over to the women with a smile glued on his face. Jenni turned back him. "What is the address of this Jasmine DuPree?"

"Why would you need that, Jenni?"

"Because I want to talk to her. It's my right."

He glanced at his wife for help but all she did was hand him paper and a pen. He wrote down an address after looking through the file for a few moments. After stuffing the paper in her purse, she said, "Is that it?"

"Isn't that enough?"

Jenni shrugged. "I want to talk to the police. Can you arrange that?"

He knew it would do no good to argue, so he nodded with resignation. There was no changing Jenni's mind when she decided something was the right thing to do. He admired her ethics and her determination, but at times she could be frustrating.

"I'll arrange it. Now, in the meantime, you must be exhausted. Why don't you let Carmen drive you home? I'll follow in our car."

Jenni started to protest, but she realized he was right; she was tired, very tired. Once in the car, Carmen put on soothing music, and Jenni laid her head on the headrest with her eyes closed.

Jasmine DuPree. The name echoed in her mind. She felt herself trembling. It had been the lowest moment of their marriage. It had been the one and only time

Shattered

they'd come close to divorce. After twenty years of marriage, she never thought she would have to deal with infidelity, but she'd been wrong.

Michael had gone on a business trip to the Bahamas, and when he'd come home, he'd been withdrawn. She knew something was wrong, but he refused to talk to her. She assumed his business hadn't gone the way he'd wanted. She didn't push him. She knew he would talk to her when he was ready.

After three nights of sleeping on the edge of the bed, as far away from Jenni as he could get, she felt him begin to shake. Then she heard the sobs. In that moment, without being told, she understood the situation with perfect clarity.

Jenni left the bed, refusing to worry about his feelings. She wouldn't comfort him. He'd been the one that had broken their vows. He followed her in the living room and told her the story even though she hadn't wanted to hear it.

He'd drunk more than he'd realized, and he'd slept with a young woman. He begged for her forgiveness. She stared at him, refusing to talk. Jenni had been numb with shock. It had never occurred to her that Michael would ever be unfaithful. She didn't know how to react. She simply stared at him.

She'd left the next morning. For a week, Jenni had holed up in the best hotel in town at Michael's expense, but in the end she agreed to stay with him for six months. She owed her marriage that much.

Chapter Three

The next six months were rough, but she was determined to give their marriage a chance. She would alternate between being angry and hurt, and just when she'd think she was beginning to get over it, then something would trigger a vision of Michael with the other woman.

Fortunately for Jenni and Michael, God had intervened through their next door neighbor, Sam. Both of them had committed their lives to God and to each other. Their marriage would never have survived without god in their lives. Their joint commitment to God had healed their marriage. Eventually, they'd worked through it and found their way back to each other, but not without a lot of anger and sorrow.

It was very cliché, but it truly had made their marriage stronger after she'd learned to trust again. They'd both learned that nothing was more important to the two of them than their marriage and their life together, and they had both spent the last six years proving that to each other every day.

Theirs was not a 50–50 marriage but a 100–100 marriage. Each was completely devoted to the other. That is why all of this had thrown her into a complete tailspin. And now they would have her believe that he had been planning to leave her for Jasmine DuPree.

She turned to Carmen.

"I don't believe it," Jenni cried out with anger.

Without a moment's hesitation, Carmen answered, "Neither do I." She nodded her head for emphasis. "I don't believe any of it."

Jenni turned to look at her friend. "He did know her, Carmen." She spoke softly. "He did have a one-night stand with her, but that was many years ago. He made a mistake and I forgave him."

Carmen swerved toward the curb as she turned to look at Jenni. She overcompensated and almost hit the car beside her, but she regained control of the car. She shrugged and patted Jenni's shoulder. "It happens. The important thing is that you got through it."

"I'm going to prove that they are wrong. He didn't do the things they said. I owe it to Michael to prove it."

"Good," Carmen answered forcefully, but she kept her eyes on the road driving more carefully than before.

"Thanks, Carmen." Jenni knew she would have continued regardless, but it was nice to have someone on her side.

There was a strange car in the driveway. Jenni looked at Carmen and shrugged. "It seems as if I have other guests."

They got out of the car and waited for Roberto. The three of them walked in to the house. There were three people sitting in her living room. They looked up with guilty faces as she opened the door.

Nicholas Peyton stood up. He was the owner of the Marshall Corporation. She had never liked him even though Michael had spent a lot of energy trying to convince her that he was a nice guy. He was just too smooth, too perfect for her. She knew the world needed people like that, but she didn't have to like them.

Chapter Three

Nicholas had on his thousand-dollar Armani suit and even though it was sweltering outside, not a strand of his coal black hair was out of place. He rushed to Jenni, grabbing her hands in an affectionate manner. She tried to pull back from him, but he held her firmly in his grip.

"Jenni, dear. I just stopped by to check on you. I just wanted you to know that no one holds you accountable for Michael's actions. I'd have been here sooner, but I knew you weren't feeling—"

She tore away from him. "Don't you touch me. I don't know why you set Michael up—but you did—because Michael would never have stolen money from you or from anyone else. Nobody will ever make me believe that he did. Get out of my house." She turned on the others sitting in the room. "All of you get out of my house."

A woman she didn't know got up from the sofa and walked to her. She put out her hand. "I am Dr. Gail Rinaldi. Your mother was worried about you, and Nicholas thought that I might be able to help. Things like this are never easy to deal with, and it shows no weakness that you need a little help." She spoke in a soft monotone that didn't match her appearance. She was muscular in a way that said she worked out in a serious manner. She had short, black hair that was shiny and vibrant. She sported a pair of glasses with large frames. Everything about her screamed confidence.

Shattered

Jenni glared at her mother, who ignored her by smoothing down her skirt and refusing to look at Jenni. "I don't need a shrink. I need to find out the truth."

"That's what I'm here to do, help you face the truth."

Jenni gave a bitter laugh. "Do you know the truth because I don't?" Jenni looked at Annie Meyers who was sitting in a chair near her mother. Annie had worked with Michael for only the past two years, but he respected her a great deal and talked about her often.

Annie looked the same as always, your typical computer nerd all grown up. Her hair was a mousy brown and was cut in a lifeless pageboy. She wore glasses that were the antithesis of fashion. It wasn't that she wasn't pretty, but she just didn't seem to be concerned about it one way or the other. Jenni had never seen Annie wear make-up. Whenever Jenni visited Michael at work, she was always dressed in an asexual business suit that did nothing to flatter her.

"What about you, Annie? Do you believe it?"

Annie looked around at the others. Her face flushed red and she looked uncomfortable. When it became obvious that no one was going to rescue her, she spoke. "I'm having a hard time believing it, Jenni." Annie wouldn't look at Nicholas Peyton. "I really am. It doesn't seem like the man I knew at all."

Dr. Rinaldi spoke in her monotone, which was beginning to infuriate Jenni. "I understand that this is difficult for all of you. All I want to do is help you feel better."

Chapter Three

Jenni's eyes and voice betrayed what she was feeling even though her words did not. "I may have been depressed, but I'm not now. Now I'm ready to deal with the facts. But first, I have to find out what the facts are, and I won't be needing you to do that, but it was so kind of you to offer your services."

Jenni saw the look that Dr. Rinaldi and her mother shared but chose to ignore it. She turned to Annie Myers and spoke in a formal tone. "Thank you for coming over, and I'm so grateful for your kind words, but I'm tired." She gave Carmen and Roberto a hug and walked upstairs without acknowledging the others.

Once upstairs, she paced around her room trying to figure out what was going on. Something didn't feel right. Why had those people been in her house with her mother? Her head hurt. She didn't want to think about any of it.

It was Nicholas's company that the police were saying Michael stole from. So why would Nicholas want to help her? Yet, he sat in her living room pretending to be worried about her and wanting to help her. It didn't make sense. The throbbing worsened.

She needed some aspirin. She opened her door. She could hear that infuriating monotone of the doctor's droning on and on. She moved closer to hear the words.

"You must understand, she's had a great shock and she isn't ready to accept the truth, but she's making progress. Just the fact that she is up now is a good sign.

Shattered

Denial is a normal step in the grieving process. Her anger is also normal."

Carmen's voice carried above the others. "But maybe she's right. Maybe Michael wasn't the one that embezzled the money." Jenni smiled.

The doctor's tone was dismissive. "I don't know anything about that. I'm just going on what Nicholas told me. The legal proof is not my concern, but the health of Jenni is. I think she needs to go somewhere to rest for a while where she can deal with all these feelings in a safe way."

Jenni wondered what that meant; she moved closer. They wanted to keep her from finding out the truth. She waited, hoping her mother would tell them no, but instead she heard her mother agreeing. Jenni put a hand to her throbbing temples. It was hard to focus. Words floated up the stairs.

Let her go to the police station to see the proof...
If she refuses to go...
Don't worry about...
Won't be a problem...

She wouldn't let them stop her from finding the truth, but first she needed to get rid of the blinding headache. She gulped down several aspirin and walked back to her bedroom.

She lay down and began praying the same prayer that she'd prayed that morning. *Please God, give me strength.* She fell asleep repeating the prayer over and over.

Chapter Four

When Jenni awoke, the headache was gone. She thought about the things she'd heard earlier. It was hard to believe that they'd been serious. They couldn't force her to go somewhere that she didn't want to go. She was an adult. She had a right to make her own decisions.

Why was Nicholas Peyton acting like he was so concerned for her well-being? She had a hard time believing that he was sincere. If she were Nicolas and believed that her husband had embezzled from his company, she would be anything but kind and caring to his wife. He hadn't come to her house because he was worried about her. He was there because he was worried about something else.

She looked at the clock; it was after three in the morning, but her mind was racing. She wouldn't be able to go back to sleep. She turned on her light and dialed

Shattered

Carmen's house knowing that Carmen would answer, not Roberto. Roberto, according to Carmen, could sleep through a tornado if she didn't nudge him awake.

The phone was picked up before it finished the first ring. Carmen's whispered voice came on the other end of the phone line.

"Hello."

"It's me."

"Just a minute," came the whispered response. A few moments passed, and then Carmen was back talking softly, but not whispering any longer. "OK, I took the phone out in the hall so I wouldn't wake Robbie. What's wrong?"

"I heard what they were saying this afternoon. They're going to make me go some place I don't want to go."

"They're just worried about you. The doctor thinks she can help you."

"I don't need help. I need to find out the truth, to prove that they're lying about Michael. You said you would help me."

"And I will."

"You can't let them take me away."

"I don't think anyone is going to force you to go. They are just worried about you."

"Are you sure? Because it sounded that way to me."

"The doctor just told your mother to try and convince you to go to some clinic for awhile to get some rest."

Chapter Four

Jenni rolled her eyes. "That's all I've been doing for the past few months. You'll go to the police station in the morning with me?"

"Of course. I'll pick you up. No one is trying to hurt you; they're just worried."

In the morning, Carmen kept her word and picked Jenni up to go to the police station. She tried to talk about trivial matters, but Jenni barely acknowledged her, so Carmen gave up and thought about what had happened at her own breakfast table that morning.

She'd been overseeing breakfast for the kids when Robbie came down dressed for the day, but not looking all that happy. "I heard the phone ring in the middle of the night." His dark brown eyes gave her a piercing look. She avoided looking back by turning to the sink and washing dishes.

"It was Jenni. She wanted to talk."

"About what? Stop washing those dishes and look at me." The kids stopped fussing with each other and looked up, intrigued by the tone of their father's voice. They rarely saw their parents argue.

Carmen flung her head back in a gesture of defiance and turned with hands on hips to glare at him. She motioned for the kids to leave the room, which they did without protest. They knew their mother when she was angry.

Her accent was thickened by her anger; she turned back to her husband. "What do you think she wanted

Shattered

to talk about, Robbie? Her dead husband, the awful things they are saying, the fact that people are acting as if she is crazy. Pick any of them; she has a lot on her mind right now."

He took a step back in an unconscious move to defuse the situation, talking in a calming tone. "I know that, Carmen. I just wondered why she called so late. Did she want something?"

"Yes, she wanted me to act like her friend. Is that all right with you, macho man?"

"Of course, of course. Did she say exactly what she wanted?"

"She's afraid they are going to force her to go away."

"But you know it's best for her. It's the safest place for her right now."

"What do you mean the safest place? Is she in danger?" Her eyes filled with concern. She had promised to help Jenni, but she didn't want her to get hurt.

"No, no. I just meant that she seems so confused and agitated. I wouldn't want her to hurt herself. She's been through a lot."

"What are you saying? Do you think she's suicidal?"

He gave a shrug. "It's possible. The doctor said loved ones of suicide victims often attempt to do the same."

Carmen spun around and demanded to know. "When did she say that? I didn't hear her."

Roberto looked surprised at the question. He hadn't wanted Carmen to know what he'd done the past after-

Chapter Four

noon. She would be enraged if she knew. He ignored her question.

"I just don't want you interfering." He picked up his coffee cup.

"Interfering with what?" Her hands were back on her hips.

He looked at his watch. "I've got to go. I'll meet you at the station."

Carmen picked up Jenni at her house, and they drove directly to the police station. As they walked into the station, it was hard for Jenni not to remember the last time she'd been there. Roberto walked up to the car and smiled at his wife and Jenni. She willed it to be that day and things would end differently. Roberto interrupted her thoughts.

"I've arranged for you to look at the documents, and Detective Lambert will be there to answer any questions. You don't have to do this, Jenni. Just go home and forget about it. Trust me when I tell you it would be better to just go home." He touched her arm. Carmen gave him a strange look and wondered why he was so anxious for her to stop pursuing the truth.

Jenni smiled. "I don't have a choice."

Detective Lambert turned out to be Detective Wanda Lambert. She didn't look much like a police officer. She just barely squeaked by the height requirement. Her blonde hair was cut short and stuck up at odd angles all over her head. She was in jeans and a tie-dyed T-shirt that had a peace symbol on it.

Shattered

Detective Lambert gave an apologetic smile and gestured at her clothes. "Sorry about this. I'm doing a little undercover work and I need to fit in. Mrs. Hamilton, I am so sorry for your loss." She sounded sincere. "I was the one who arrested your husband. I feel just horrible about what happened."

Jenni tried to smile back but couldn't. Her face felt frozen. Her throat had become dry. She felt flushed and hot. "Could I get something to drink?"

Detective Lambert motioned to a small corner table that held several different types of soda, juice, and coffee. After everyone was settled, Detective Lambert looked at Jenni. "How do you want to do this? Do you want to look at the information, or do you want me to explain it as we look through it?"

"I would like you tell me about the day you arrested my husband."

It was quiet in the room. Carmen looked at her hands, Roberto was looking at the ceiling, and Detective Lambert looked at the floor.

After a few moments, Detective Lambert began to speak. "I had conferred with Mr. Peyton several times, so he knew an arrest would be occurring. I called him the previous night to tell him that it would happen the next day. Mr. Peyton arranged a meeting with Mr. Hamilton, and they were in Mr. Peyton's office when I arrived."

Chapter Four

Jenni felt a surge of anger, but not surprise that Nicholas Peyton had helped to ambush Michael. She suppressed her anger; she needed to focus on the information, not the feelings.

"Mr. Hamilton appeared to be stunned when I walked in and read him his rights but offered no resistance."

"Was anyone else in the office?"

Detective Lambert shook her head. "No, just Mr. Peyton and Mr. Hamilton."

"Did you search him when you arrested him?"

"Yes."

"So, he didn't have the pills on him when you arrested him?"

"No." Lambert shook her head and didn't look happy about the direction the questions were heading.

"Then, how did he get the pills?" Jenni looked at the three people in the room, waiting for an answer. No one spoke. Jenni asked, "Do you think that he just carried them around with him all the time, just in case he wanted to kill himself?"

"I don't know, Mrs. Hamilton. I've tried to figure that out, but I haven't been able to come with an explanation that makes sense. It bothered me, but I've been told the investigation is closed."

Jenni changed topics. "Who knew that Michael was going to be arrested that day?"

"Mr. Peyton, myself, and my boss."

"Anyone else?"

Shattered

"Not that I know of, but certainly Mr. Peyton could have confided in others. I have no way of knowing that." Detective Lambert shrugged.

Jenni felt a rush of anger at her apathy but kept it in check. She was trying not to alienate the woman. She forced herself to talk in a slow deliberate tone. "Did Mr. Peyton talk to Michael about the embezzlement before you arrived?"

"No, I don't believe so."

"What happened after that?"

"We got in the squad car and left. I do remember him complaining that his stomach hurt during the drive, but I just chalked it up to nerves."

"Why would Michael complain if he knew he had taken the pills?" she demanded of the people sitting at the table. "Someone gave him those pills without him knowing it."

Detective Lambert ignored Jenni's question and kept talking. "At the station he called you, and then I went to get him something to drink. When I went back into the room, he had collapsed. I started CPR as we waited for the ambulance."

Jenni closed her eyes. She could see Michael on the floor and Wanda Lambert bending over him trying to save him. She forced her breathing to slow down. As she opened her eyes she saw the others watching her. Jenni hated the pity that she saw in their eyes. She smiled

Chapter Four

and said with as much dignity as she could muster, "Thank you for trying to help him."

The room was still again. Roberto cleared his throat and all the women turned their eyes toward him. He had nothing to say, so he just looked back at them.

The detective took charge of the meeting again. "I only wished I'd been able to help him. It's so sad when people overreact to getting arrested. It's a horrible thing but not as horrible as taking your life."

Jenni raised her eyes and met the detective's and in a quiet voice said, "I don't believe my husband took his own life. There is more to this story, and I plan to find the truth. No one else seems to care about the truth but I do. It doesn't make sense. Michael didn't know he would be arrested that morning, so why would he have taken those drugs? He didn't have them on him when you searched him, so he couldn't have taken them after you arrested him. Someone else gave him those drugs and I intend to find out who that was."

To Jenni, it seemed obvious that someone who knew Michael would be arrested that day gave him the drugs. Someone like Nicholas Peyton. Nicholas wouldn't have been the first person to embezzle money from his own company and then blame it on others.

Wanda Lambert forced herself to be quiet; she had her own unanswered questions but had been told not to pursue them. She grabbed the folder and opened it.

Shattered

"When we were contacted by Mr. Peyton, we investigated all the people in that department. All the evidence pointed to Mr. Hamilton. His signature was on all the documents that showed funds being transferred, and then there was the passport and visa we found. Then the Bahamian government informed us that he was listed as a co-owner on two different pieces of property."

The detective began reaching for papers from the file, and Jenni hunched over to get a better look at them. Detective Lambert gave Jenni a sympathetic smile, took a deep breath, and began.

She showed Jenni a variety of documents that verified the information about the embezzling that had taken place. She handed Jenni more documents. "The money was transferred to an account in the Cayman Islands. We are not able to get information about that account according to International Banking Laws."

"We believe Jasmine DuPree was your husband's lover, and he was planning on moving to Freeport to be with her."

"What makes you think that?"

"The local police questioned her, and she admitted that Michael was planning to move down there with her, but she hadn't realized he was stealing money to do it. She was cooperative."

"So, what proof do you have, or is her word all the proof you have?"

"She had no reason to lie."

Chapter Four

Jenni refused to believe that Michael had been betraying her for years with Jasmine DuPree. He could have left at any time if that was what he chose to do. She had never tried to force him to stay. He was the one who had sworn over and over that this woman meant nothing to him

"Is there anything else?" Jenni asked, forcing her eyes to meet the detective's eyes. Jenni's eyes challenged and Lambert's eyes sympathized knowing that this would be difficult for any wife to deal with but impossible for a newly-widowed woman who couldn't confront her husband with his betrayal.

"No."

"It looks like it's all circumstantial to me."

"He authorized the payments to the bogus company time and time again. That is not circumstantial. That is a fact."

Jenni looked around the table trying to garner support for her position. "That doesn't mean anything, not really." She knew that sounded lame, but she believed in her husband and his innocence.

Jenni stood up and offered her hand to Detective Lambert. "Thank you for your time, Detective."

Chapter Five

Not a word passed between Carmen and Jenni as they drove home. Jenni laid her head back with eyes closed willing the throbbing in her head to disappear. She tried to breathe through the pain but it remained. Several times, Carmen turned to her friend to say something comforting but stopped because she didn't know what to say.

Once they were in the driveway, Carmen turned to Jenni and said, "Jenni, maybe you should take a break and go away for a while. Just forget about all of this and worry about yourself instead. Pamper yourself, go to the beach and read books."

Jenni sat in the car playing with her wedding band knowing that the letters "gmfl" were there. That had been Michael's promise to her, and she didn't believe he had any intention of breaking his promise. Jenni shook her head trying to be angry with her friend but not quite

Shattered

able to feel anything at the moment. "I know it sounded bad, Carmen, and I don't know how to explain it. I just know he didn't do it, and I owe it to Michael to prove that. What would you do if it were Roberto?"

"I know, I know what you're saying." Carmen gave her a hug. Carmen knew she would support her friend; it didn't matter what the facts were.

Jenni walked in the door wondering what the rest of the day would hold. Her mother was on the other side of the door and gave her a hug. It was meant to comfort and encourage her, but nothing could do that.

Her mother hovered over Jenni giving her coffee and cookies, but all Jenni wanted was to be alone. Jenni set the coffee on the glass-topped coffee table and gave her mother a smile trying to show her how well she was doing.

"Mom, I can't tell you how much it's meant to me to have you here helping me through this, but it's time you get back to your own life. You only live a few miles away, so I can always call you whenever I need you."

Beth's hands fluttered. "Dr. Rinaldi doesn't think that would be such a good idea, Jenni."

"I don't care what Dr. Rinaldi thinks is a good idea. She is not my doctor."

"She thinks the two of us should go away for a while. Mr. Peyton offered you the use of his beach house."

"I'm not going to the lake or anywhere else. I have things to do."

Chapter Five

"What do you need to do, Jenni?" Beth sat on the couch, giving her daughter a hard look, trying to decide what to do. Her crossed legs bounced unconsciously as she took a deep drag on her cigarette.

"I have to prove that Michael was innocent. I do not need to go sit by a lake and act like I'm feeble-minded."

"You are not the police; that is their job, not yours."

"Well, they haven't done a very good job of it so far. They've decided he's guilty and as far as they're concerned the case is closed." Jenni took a deep breath and pushed back the tears that were pressing against her eyelids. "That is not acceptable to me."

After a few more drags on her cigarette, Beth Collins asked her daughter, "What exactly do you plan to do?"

Jenni was beginning to wonder why her mother was asking so many questions. She looked suspiciously at the coffee, and her mind flashed back to the tranquilizers that her mother had been feeding without her knowledge. Jenni sat the coffee down quickly, spilling it on her hand.

"Is your hand OK?" Her mother fluttered around Jenni like a moth around a street light.

"It's fine. I was just wondering if maybe you drugged the coffee since I wouldn't take those pills."

Beth took a step back, hurt by the accusation. She was on the verge of tears when she spoke. "I did no such thing. Why are you acting like I'm trying to hurt you? I'm your mother. I just want to help you. The doctor said the pills would be good for you."

Shattered

"She's not my doctor."

"I know but I just wanted to help."

"Good, then help me by going home now." Jenni softened her tone not wanting to be hateful. "I just need to be alone. You've taken good care of me, but now it's time I start taking care of myself again."

Beth Collins looked doubtfully at her daughter. It wouldn't hurt to wait. She thought of the papers sitting in her purse. Mr. Peyton and Dr. Rinaldi had been so helpful, but Beth didn't want to use the papers unless it was absolutely necessary.

"Fine, I'll go home, but you have to promise to call me every day, just so I know that you're all right."

"OK, OK." Jenni would have agreed to anything at that point. She just wanted her mother out of the house so she could do what she needed to do, which was to prove Michael's innocence.

Jenni breathed a sigh of relief after her mother left. It had taken a while for Beth to gather her things and still she had been reluctant to leave. She'd cried and fussed over Jenni but finally kept her promise and went home. Jenni threw herself down on the nearest chair and breathed deeply.

This was the first time she had been truly alone since Michael had died. The quiet was what she noticed. It was a different kind of quiet than before. She'd always enjoyed the silence, it had been a tranquil respite, but this quiet had such a finality to it that it made her shud-

Chapter Five

der. She wouldn't hear the door opening or Michael calling her name again or his off-key singing to the radio.

She forced the maudlin thoughts away. She'd done that long enough. Now it was time for action. She would prove Michael's innocence. She just had to decide how to do that. The logical place to start would be Michael's job. Someone there knew the truth, and Jenni was determined to find that person.

Jenni called Annie Meyers and arranged a time for her to pick up Michael's things. She picked up her purse and keys and left the house. She couldn't stand the quiet for one minute longer.

The Marshall Corporation manufactured a variety of parts that eventually ended up in cars, trains, and even airplanes. Michael had taken a pay cut to take the job, but in return they had offered him stock options, and those options had made Michael and Jenni richer than they could ever have imagined. They'd had plenty of money. He hadn't needed to steal from the company.

Michael loved his job at the Marshall Corporation. He was able to use his MBA along with his engineering degree. A major portion of his job was helping to develop the bids for individual jobs. He liked to explain to Jenni that it was an art form to get the bid just right. A bid large enough to give the company a healthy profit and low enough to win the bid from their competitors.

Jenni sat at Michael's desk looking around his office at the Marshall Corporation. One wall was decorated with awards from various professional and community organizations. One wall was made entirely of glass, which had allowed Michael to look out at the pond and trees. The other two walls were a testament to Michael's life.

It was a gallery of pictures of family, friends, and co-workers. Michael had fancied himself an amateur photographer. Many were snapshots, but he'd had his favorites blown up to larger sizes; all were framed, showing that the memories were treasured. Jenni walked over and began taking them down, packing them in a box that Annie Meyers had found for her. Jenni didn't notice the tears, but Annie had. She discreetly left the room so Jenni could have privacy.

Michael had spent so much of his time in his office. He'd given his heart and soul to help make this company successful, and now he had apparently given his life as well. For Jenni, there could be no other explanation. Someone here at the Marshall Corporation had set Michael up.

Perhaps the company wasn't doing as well as she'd been led to believe. Maybe Nicholas needed the money for his extravagant lifestyle. It would have been easy enough for him to set Michael up, so that it looked as if Michael had stolen the money, not Nicholas.

After the pictures were packed, she went through Michael's desk but found nothing to point her in the right direction. File cabinets were locked, and when she asked to have them opened, the temp secretary sitting

Chapter Five

at the desk said she didn't have the authority to let Jenni in the files. Annie Meyers was called.

She walked in looking angry. She was in a gray business suit that would have been stylish except that it was two sizes too big. She greeted Jenni with a hug and then turned on the secretary.

"Of course Mrs. Hamilton has a right to look through the files to make sure there isn't anything personal in them. Michael might have personal papers or items in the file cabinet."

The secretary stuttered, "I didn't mean anything by it. I just thought that she wasn't allowed to go through the files. You know, I mean, after what happened."

Annie Meyers gave the secretary a cold stare through the thick lenses of her glasses. "As far as I'm concerned, nothing happened except that her husband died, and she has a right to any of his personal items that he might have kept here in his office. So, I would appreciate it if you would open the files so she can make sure she has all of her husband's things." Annie waited a beat and then added, "Now."

The secretary dropped the keys in her haste to please Annie. She was apologetic as she bent to pick them up. Jenni felt sorry for her but was glad to see someone finally defending Michael. Annie grabbed the keys from the secretary and marched into the office without another word. The secretary looked after her worriedly.

Annie turned back to the secretary and pointed to the boxes that were filled. "Arrange for someone to take these out to Mrs. Hamilton's car."

The secretary started to say something but changed her mind. She muttered, "Of course."

Annie shut the door after Jenni and gave her a smile. "Just need to show them who's the boss every now and then. I'm sorry she was so rude."

Annie's dark gray suit contrasted with the black one she'd worn at Jenni's house, but the suit did nothing to emphasize her sexuality. Her hair was still in that unflattering pageboy, and she wore no make-up or jewelry. Jenni wondered what kind of a social life Annie had.

"So, you're going to be the boss, now."

Annie rolled her eyes. "Probably not. They just gave me the position temporarily until they can find a replacement for Michael. They've decided to conduct a search."

"Why not you?"

"Oh, I don't know. I'm fine as an assistant, but you know about the 'glass ceiling.' I've probably gone as far as I can go with this company. I'll be turning in my resignation as soon as they hire a replacement." She rolled her eyes.

"That doesn't seem right. I know Michael trusted your judgment. He'd want you to take over. I'm sure of it."

She gave a shrug. "It's just a part of life when you work in a male-dominated business."

"Do they know you're interested in the position?"

Chapter Five

She nodded. "I talked to them about it and they said all the right words. One must be politically correct these days, you know, but they still wanted to do a search. If they wanted me, they wouldn't go to the expense of a search." Annie gave a shrug.

"That's not right. You've worked hard here. You deserve the promotion." Jenni turned toward the files and began shuffling through them. "It doesn't sound as if you believe the charges against Michael."

"Of course not. It's ridiculous. Michael was one of the good guys. I wish I could find someone like him to marry."

Jenni smiled. "You would be lucky if you did. He was a wonderful husband. I'm not saying our marriage was perfect but it was better than most."

"Jenni, I've worked with Michael for almost two years. I never saw any sign at all that he was dishonest." Annie's eyes, magnified through the thick glasses, blinked several times.

"Who would be in a position to make it look like he did those things, Annie?" Jenni held her breath, not wanting to scare Annie off. Annie didn't say anything for a few seconds.

"I don't know. I suppose it could have been any of the vice-presidents or even someone in this department."

"Or the CEO?"

Annie looked surprised at the question. "Nicholas? I suppose so, but why would he want to, it's his company."

Shattered

Jenni was hasty to reassure Annie. "I'm not accusing him. I just wanted to get an idea who would be able to set Michael up."

Annie took a few minutes to think about it as Jenni searched through the files. "Now that I'm thinking about it, it could have been most anyone that had access to the financial records. We're more lax than we should be about access to our files."

Jenni straightened up from her search. "Is there anyone that you might suspect?"

Annie looked around the office, almost as if someone might be listening. She started to say something and then thought better of it. "No, I can't imagine anyone here doing something like that. Sorry."

Jenni smiled. She stood up and dusted off her hands. "I guess that's it. Thanks, I'll just go in and say goodbye to Nicholas before I leave." Jenni didn't really want to see Nicholas but she hoped she might get some information from him.

"He told me to tell you he left for a meeting." Annie gave her a quick hug. "Let me know if there's anything I can do."

Jenni assessed the situation and decided to take a chance. "There is something you can do."

"Sure, what is it?"

"Just let me know if you come across anything odd."

Annie assured her she would call if she found anything odd. On Jenni's way outside, she could feel

Chapter Five

someone's eyes on her. She turned to look back. She looked up and squinted against the blinding reflection of the sun against the glass building. She saw a figure looking out of the window. She couldn't see anything but a silhouette. She knew it was paranoid to think the person was watching her, but just the same, she did.

As she got in her car, she noticed that Nicholas Peyton's car was in the same parking place as when she arrived. He hadn't gone anywhere. She could imagine why he hadn't wanted to see her.

The silhouette watched Jenni Hamilton walk to her car. When Jenni turned around, the person flinched and wanted to move away from the window but knew that it was impossible for Jenni to see a face clearly. *Hopefully, Jenni would go home and forget all about trying to figure out why Michael died. Jenni was too nice a person to have anything happen to her, but of course Michael had been one of the good guys, too. But business was business.*

The figure moved over to the telephone and hit some numbers. "She's gone. She asked a few people a few questions but nothing important. I'll keep an eye on her, but I'm sure she's harmless, just a confused housewife who refuses to believe that her dead husband was going to leave her for another woman. Everyone just feels sorry for her. I'm sure there is nothing to worry about at all."

Jenni was exhausted by the time she got home. She walked out of the summer heat and into the coolness of an air-conditioned house, tossed her purse, slipped off

Shattered

her shoes, and lay down on the couch. She was awakened sometime later by a ringing. She went to the phone but realized it was the doorbell. She debated about not answering but knew that it was probably her mother checking up on her, so she opened the door.

Roberto and Carmen were standing at the door with a bucket of fried chicken. Carmen gave her a hug. "We just wanted to make sure you would eat tonight, and then we'll be on our way."

Jenni opened the door wider to welcome them in.

"Did my mother tell you to come and check up on me?"

Carmen's brown eyes twinkled with laughter. "What do you think?"

After they were sitting at the table and eating the greasy chicken with their fingers, Roberto said, "I heard you went to Marshall today."

"How did you know that?"

"Nicholas happened to mention it when we were talking on the phone."

"Did he also happen to mention that he pretended he was out of the building so he wouldn't have to talk to me?"

Roberto's dark brown eyes reflected confusion and surprise. "I can't imagine why he would do that. You must be confused. Why would he mention that you were even there if that were the case?"

"To not bring any suspicion to him."

Chapter Five

Roberto stopped chewing and looked at Jenni. "You think Nicholas is responsible for Michael's death?"

Jenni shrugged. "It's possible. It makes sense. He has access to the records. He knew Michael was going to be arrested that day, so he could have drugged him before the police came. If Michael had lived, he'd have been able to prove that he'd been set up and probably been able to find out the guilty party."

"Why would Nicholas steal his own money, Jenni?" Roberto looked at Carmen, but she refused to meet his eyes. She kept eating her chicken.

"I don't know, but I'm going to find out. I'm going to fly to Freeport to talk to Jasmine DuPree. Maybe, she'll be able to tell me what's going on."

Carmen and Roberto both tried to talk her out of her plan, but the more they argued against it, the more positive Jenni became that it was the right thing to do.

Once they were in the car, Roberto grabbed his cell phone. Carmen listened to the call with growing horror.

"We just left Jenni's house. She's planning on taking a trip to the Bahamas tomorrow. We tried to talk her out of it but she refused to listen to reason. She has to be stopped. She can't go down there. Good, you do what's necessary to stop her."

Carmen pulled over and began to flail at Roberto as she cried and screamed at him. "What are you doing? You're part of this. I can't believe this. Jenni's right. Michael was murdered." She didn't know what to do,

Shattered

so she jumped out of the car and began running back to Jenni's house. She had to warn her.

Roberto jumped out of the car and chased Carmen. He tried to calm her, but she kept hitting at him all the while crying. She was the one whose husband had betrayed her. Roberto engulfed her with his arms, and she sagged against his chest crying.

"Baby, baby," he crooned to her, "you misunderstood what I was doing. Let me explain." He guided her back to their car. She leaned against the car, feeling the heat of the metal against her back. Roberto leaned against the car with his arms still around her.

"I was talking to Beth. Yesterday, Beth went to a judge and got a court order that allowed her to hospitalize Jenni if necessary. I was just calling Beth. I wasn't trying to hurt Jenni."

"How could you do that to Jenni?"

"How could I not? She's had a shock and she isn't dealing with it in a rational way. I would never forgive myself if something happened to her. I owe it to Michael to make sure she's OK. I have to keep her safe even if she gets mad at me."

Carmen began crying in earnest, not sure if it was from relief or anger. "I'm so sorry. When I heard you talking like that I thought you were trying to hurt her." She covered his face with kisses as she apologized.

"It's my fault," Roberto said as he comforted his wife. "I should have explained what I was doing before I made

Chapter Five

the call. It's not always easy to do the right thing, but I'm sure Michael would want me to protect Jenni." Roberto helped Carmen into the passenger side of the car, worried that Carmen didn't believe his explanation.

Jenni was upstairs packing when she heard the car pull in. She'd already arranged a flight for the next day. A quick glance out the window told her it was her mother's car, which was not surprising.

When she opened the door, not only was her mother on the doorstep, but so was Nicholas Peyton and Dr. Rinaldi. Three strange men stood behind them. Before Jenni could ask them what they wanted, they pushed past her and into the house. Dr. Rinaldi was carrying a black medical bag.

Jenni looked at her mother for an explanation. Beth Collins looked every bit her sixty-eight years that night. Her eyes were outlined in red and her hair looked as if she'd forgotten to comb it. She couldn't look her daughter in the eye as she spoke.

"Jenni, dear. We need to talk to you."

Jenni's heart fluttered, but she refused to show her anxiety. "I didn't invite any of you here, so please leave. Mother, I will talk to you tomorrow. I'm busy right now."

Dr. Rinaldi spoke up. "I'm sorry, we can't do that, Jenni."

As the doctor spoke, the three men and Nicholas formed a loose circle around Jenni. Her mother remained outside of the circle, shredding a tissue and looking terrified. Jenni had a sick feeling in the pit of her stomach. She couldn't believe this was happening.

"Now, if you remain calm. I will explain what is happening here. Otherwise, we will do this the hard way."

"Do what?" Jenni felt panic rising up and she wanted to run but could see that she wouldn't get far. "I want all of you to leave, now." She tried to sound authoritative but failed.

"Your mother is worried about you. We're here to take you to the hospital so you can get better, Jenni." Her monotone scraped against Jenni's ears like nails on a chalkboard.

Jenni looked around wildly. Panic overtook her. "Hospital. I don't need a hospital. I want you all to leave." Jenni could hear her mother whimpering.

The doctor motioned for the men to step closer, tightening the circle as they did so. Jenni's chest tightened as the circle tightened around her. She looked out at her mother, but her mother refused to meet her eyes. Jenni's heart was racing and her palms were sweaty.

"Mom, don't do this," she pleaded.

The doctor spoke, "We aren't here to hurt you. We want to help you." The men took a few steps closer to Jenni.

"You can't do this. You have no right." Jenni lunged forward, but two of the men grabbed her. The doctor opened her black bag and pulled out a syringe. Jenni kicked at the men but to no avail. The doctor walked toward her, carefully holding the syringe as she did.

Chapter Five

Jenni waited until the doctor came closer and kicked at her. Her foot landed against the doctor's stomach. The syringe dropped from her hand and anger flashed in the doctor's eyes before she regained control.

Jenni screamed at her mother, "Mom, don't let them do this. They will kill me. They killed Michael. Don't let them kill me. Stop them, Mom, stop them."

Her mother looked like a rabbit caught in headlights. Nicholas Peyton moved to her mother's side and touched her arm in a comforting manner. The two men laid Jenni on the floor as if she were a feather, even though she was struggling with all her strength. She felt the needle jab into her backside, and then the panic subsided. Then she lost consciousness.

Chapter Six

Jenni opened her eyes, confused and groggy, not quite able to focus. She attempted to sit up but something stopped her. She could not move her arms or her legs. She looked around trying to understand why she couldn't sit up. She saw that she was lying in a hospital bed with restraints on both her legs and her arms.

The fogginess was replaced by panic as she remembered the scene at her house. Jenni still felt the jab of the needle. She struggled against the restraints until exhaustion overtook her. She lay in the bed, panting.

After she'd calmed down, Jenni looked around the room. It looked like an ordinary bedroom, not a hospital room. That doctor had said they were taking her to a hospital, but this wasn't a hospital. These people murdered Michael and now they would kill her, and her mother had helped them. The last thought brought a sob.

Shattered

The door creaked open and a woman moved into view. She looked to be in her mid-thirties. Her bright red hair was pulled back into a bun but curls and frizz had escaped. She was wearing a stylish pantsuit; not exactly what you would expect a nurse to wear.

She smiled at Jenni. "Would you like some water?"

Jenni nodded yes. The woman touched a button on the bed, and Jenni felt herself being moved to a sitting position. She held a glass with a straw up to Jenni's mouth and Jenni took several sips. "Thank you."

"You're welcome. Do you know where you are?"

Jenni shook her head no.

"You're at Dr. Rinaldi's private clinic. You're very lucky to have Dr. Rinaldi treating you. She's very good. You'll be feeling better in no time at all."

Jenni sensed that this woman was not out to hurt her. Maybe she could convince her to help. "No, no, I've been kidnapped. You have to help me."

The woman smiled and patted Jenni's hand. "No, you haven't been kidnapped. I saw the court order myself and it was signed by a judge. Your mother is just trying to help you."

"Court order, mother, judge." Jenni mumbled the words, straining to make sense.

The woman pushed back a few strands of red hair and smiled encouragingly at Jenni. "That's right. No one wants to hurt you. Your mom was worried about you, so she went to court and the judge agreed that

Chapter Six

you needed a little help to get through this problem you're having."

"You don't understand. Somebody killed my husband, and they want to stop me from finding out who it was."

"As I understand it, your husband killed himself, Jenni." The woman didn't say it unkindly, just as a statement of fact, but Jenni flinched at the words. "I don't want to be cruel, but the sooner you accept the truth, the sooner you'll start to get better. I know it must be a horrible thing, but you want to get better, don't you? Are you hungry?"

Tears fell from Jenni's eyes. This woman wouldn't help her. She shook her head no at the offer of food.

"Where's my mom?"

"I'm sure she'll be up soon to visit with you."

"Where's Dr. Rinaldi?"

"She'll see you tomorrow. She likes to give the clients time to get settled. I think you ought to eat. The food here is very good."

Food was the last thing Jenni wanted, but she wanted the woman to see that she was being reasonable. If she could just show the woman that she wasn't crazy, maybe she could convince her to help her.

The woman came back in a few minutes with an omelet and a glass of milk. Jenni took a few bites to please this woman. She'd asked to have her hands freed, but the woman had only smiled and said not yet. The

Shattered

woman brought out a bedpan, which Jenni had no choice but to use, no matter how humiliating.

The woman left and Jenni closed her eyes. The tension oozed out of her body, and she felt herself falling asleep. The bed was lying flat when she awakened. She had no idea what time of the day it was. The windows had dark blinds on them that allowed no light to seep in. There was a soft light in the room coming from a source she couldn't see from the position she was in.

Jenni understood that panicking would not help, but it didn't stop her. She closed her eyes and prayed. She felt calmness replacing the anxiety. She heard the door creak and opened her eyes to see Dr. Rinaldi entering. Jenni looked at her captor.

She was probably in her forties, but it was hard to tell because she was in such good shape. She was of average height, but there wasn't an ounce of fat on her muscular body. It was obvious that she worked out a great deal and indeed was wearing bicycle shorts and a tank top at the moment. Her outfit accentuated her strength. Her dark red-framed glasses hid her eyes.

"Good morning, Jenni. I hope you slept well. Now, I know you must be upset, but let me assure you that no one wants to hurt you. I'm here to help you get healthy, and then you can go home."

Jenni looked at her for a moment and then turned away as much as she could with the restraints on. It was easy for the doctor to talk about going home; she had her freedom.

Chapter Six

"This will go much easier and faster if you talk to me."

Jenni glared at the doctor.

"I understand your hostility, Jenni, but you must understand we only want to help you."

Just then the woman from last night entered carrying a tray with an assortment of food. Her red hair was still pulled back, but again curls had escaped, softening the hairstyle. "A little grouchy this morning, are we? This food should make you feel better." She set the tray down. "I forgot to introduce myself last night. I'm Lorena and I'm your nurse. I'll be in a little later to check on you."

"Don't go, Lorena. Please, she's drugging me. That's how she killed my husband. Please, help me."

Lorena and Dr. Rinaldi shared a look. "Jenni, I never even met your husband. Why would I want to kill him?"

"I don't know but . . . but . . ." She stopped in midsentence. She knew she couldn't convince Lorena. Lorena left the room with a worried glance at Jenni.

Dr. Rinaldi pressed the button on the bed, and Jenni slowly moved up to a sitting position.

"So, are you hungry?"

Jenni was hungry, but she didn't want to give Dr. Rinaldi the satisfaction. She closed her eyes in an attempt to ignore the doctor. Even though her eyes were closed, she could smell the aroma.

Dr. Rinaldi smiled knowing that it was only a matter of time before Jenni succumbed to her appetite. That

Shattered

was one of the reasons Dr. Rinaldi insisted on a chef instead of a cook at her clinic. That and the fact that most of her clients were extremely rich and could well afford the additional expense.

Dr. Rinaldi picked up the spoon and held it under Jenni's nose in a bizarre version of the airplane game. Unfortunately, it worked and Jenni did eat several bites of the minestrone soup. It was made fragrant by basil and garlic and was loaded with an assortment of fresh vegetables. In spite of her good intentions, Jenni ate most of the soup with the doctor's help.

Dr. Rinaldi continued to talk as she fed Jenni. She used a soft singsong voice. Jenni refused to listen but could feel herself relaxing in spite of herself. She laid her head on the pillow and closed her eyes. From far away she could hear the doctor talk about not feeling angry, about being accepting, and then Jenni floated away dreaming that she was on a cloud far away.

She was alone when she awoke and again had no idea of the time, but her stomach was rumbling, which meant she had slept for some time. She resolved not to eat again, positive that the food was being drugged. Lorena popped her head in the door.

"So, you're awake, sleepyhead. You must have been exhausted the way you keep sleeping. Your family was right when they said you needed to rest."

"I'm not tired. I'm getting drugged."

Chapter Six

"No, you're not, sweetie. I'm in charge of the drugs, and you've only been given a small amount of a tranquilizer. Certainly not enough to account for all this sleeping. Sleep deprivation can do strange things to a mind. It can induce paranoia. You'll be feeling better before you know it."

Lorena helped her use the bedpan again. Jenni tried to convince Lorena that she was being drugged, but Lorena just scoffed, kept calling her sweetie, and told her she would be all better soon. Jenni gave up and remained uncommunicative to Lorena's attempts to make conversation.

She fell asleep once again and dreamed that she heard Dr. Rinaldi. When she opened her eyes, Dr. Rinaldi was sitting beside her bed.

"If you want to eat, I'll take your hand restraints off, and as long as you're good, I'll leave them off."

There were a lot of things she could have said but it wouldn't have helped her situation, so instead Jenni just nodded.

The doctor unlocked the restraints on Jenni's hands. Jenni felt a sense of freedom at being able to move her arms. She had the urge to grab the food and throw it in Dr. Rinaldi's face but knew that would accomplish nothing but to get her back in the restraints. She understood that at this point she was not in control.

She picked up the juice and took a drink. It was freshly squeezed orange juice with a hint of pineapple

Shattered

and papaya. The doctor nodded, pleased to see her patient was adjusting.

"Good decision, Jenni," the doctor said as Jenni set the juice back down on the tray. "You can't win, so you might as well let us help you get healthy again."

"I don't need your help. I'm not crazy."

"No one thinks you're crazy. Your husband betrayed you and then killed himself, so you can't even allow yourself to be angry with him. So, instead you're angry with everyone around you. It's quite a normal reaction."

Jenni tore the cherry-filled Danish apart and enjoyed the buttery sweetness. She focused on the Danish rather than Dr. Rinaldi's words. She wouldn't listen to the words because the words were dangerous. She knew she was being drugged, but she had no choice. She had to eat and drink.

"You can't hold me against my will. That's kidnapping."

"You probably don't remember, but your mother got a court order allowing you to be hospitalized."

"This isn't a hospital."

"No, you're lucky that Mr. Peyton is so concerned about you. He's spending a lot of money to keep you here instead. This is so much more comfortable than a hospital."

"I want to go to a hospital, just a regular hospital."

The doctor gave her a severe look. She wasn't happy with Jenni's attitude. "No, Jenni. I don't think so. You're going to stay here until you're ready to accept your husband's suicide."

Chapter Six

Dr. Rinaldi was talking in that same soothing tone. Jenni felt her body relaxing. She tried to be angry with Dr. Rinaldi and her mother but instead she laid her head back against the pillow.

"Remember that. He betrayed you; you did nothing wrong. You have a right to a new, wonderful life. That's what he was going to do. He was going to leave you for that other woman and start a new life without you."

Jenni wanted to protest. The doctor was wrong. Michael loved her and hadn't done anything wrong. But Jenni felt tired, and it didn't seem important enough to get in an argument with the doctor right this moment. *Maybe later.* The doctor's voice went on and on telling her that Michael was the bad guy and she the victim. Jenni felt herself drifting away but did agree she was the victim. She just didn't know who was to blame.

She woke up with a sense of well-being that felt out of place in this place, which she considered a prison. It took her a few seconds to realize that both the arm and leg restraints had been removed. She jumped off the bed and went to the door, which, not surprisingly, was locked. She went to another door in the room that turned out to be a luxurious bathroom.

Seeing no reason not to, Jenni ran hot water in the tub and dumped in bath oils. The mirrors were soon steamed up, and she slipped into the bubbles. The water felt silky against her skin.

Shattered

Jenni felt a pang of guilt but dismissed it. She didn't want to be here, but there was no harm in enjoying a hot bath. When she reentered the bedroom, a gown and slippers sat on the bed. She put them on, and as she toweled her wet hair, she explored the bedroom.

The room was twice as large as her own bedroom. There was a couch and chair set up in one corner near a fireplace. In another corner there was a mahogany desk and chair. The room was carpeted in a pale rose shade that matched the walls.

Jenni noticed the things that were missing from the room: a telephone, a clock, and a television. The only reading materials were classics such as Dickinson, Louisa Mae Alcott, and Mark Twain. There was nothing in the room that would allow the reality of the world to intrude on her tranquility and that was fine with her. She'd had enough of the world.

A knock on the door startled Jenni. Lorena entered carrying a tray. Her red hair hung loose that day. "You slept through lunch, so I've brought you an early dinner."

"Thank you."

Lorena smiled at Jenni. "This can be a very nice place when you decide to cooperate. Think of it as a retreat. Would you like company, or would you rather be alone?"

"No, company would be nice. Can you explain why everyone is being so much nicer today than yesterday?"

Chapter Six

Jenni had been at the clinic for several days, but Lorena didn't correct her misconception.

"This isn't a prison. We only keep clients restrained when we are forced to, and they come off as soon as Dr. Rinaldi feels that it is safe to."

"So, I can leave my room?"

"Not quite yet, but I'm sure you'll earn that privilege soon." Lorena gave Jenni an encouraging pat. "Now that you're making such good progress."

After eating, Jenni felt slightly drowsy, so she lay on the bed. Dr. Rinaldi came in and began to talk. There didn't seem to be any reason for Jenni to talk. Dr. Rinaldi seemed perfectly content to be the one talking and Jenni to be the one listening. She didn't even have to listen all that closely to what Dr. Rinaldi was saying. Gail Rinaldi's voice oozed over Jenni like warm syrup on a waffle. Jenni imagined herself lying on a white beach on a soft blue day, drifting, feeling the warm sun on her face.

Dr. Gail Rinaldi left Jenni's room with a smile on her face. Things were proceeding nicely. Jenni had become an ideal patient in a very short amount of time. She wasn't resisting at all anymore. Dr. Rinaldi told herself that Jenni really did want to forget her troubles and Gail was helping her. There wasn't anything wrong with that—not really.

She entered her own office, which was sparse compared to the opulence of the clients' rooms. Gail didn't like all that fuss but knew the clients enjoyed the luxury.

Shattered

Her clients were not usually mentally ill but rather rich people whose lives had become overwhelming. It was Gail's job to help them regain the control.

She hit the speed dial on her phone.

"Hi, this is Gail. Can you talk?"

"Just one moment." Gail could hear instructions being given, apparently to an underling by the tone of the voice.

"OK, I'm back. What's wrong?"

"Nothing's wrong. I just called to give you an update. Things are going better than I'd hoped. At this rate, she should be able to go home in a few weeks."

"That is good news."

"Will I be able to see you tonight?"

"I don't know. I have a late meeting, but I can stop over afterwards, if you don't mind the time."

"To see you, sweetheart, I'd stay up all night."

"I'll meet you at the apartment then." They kept an apartment because it wouldn't be good for either of them to be seen in public together. They both had too much to lose.

Chapter Seven

Jenni's life fell into an endless pattern of eating, listening to Dr. Rinaldi as she talked on and on, and then spending most of the day reading. She saw Dr. Rinaldi several times each day. Jenni never had to talk but only to listen. The sessions usually relaxed her to the point of sleep for which she was grateful. Dr. Rinaldi was usually gone when Jenni woke up.

Slowly, Jenni's agitation began to lessen. She thought less and less about Michael, and at times that bothered her, but then she would remember how awful the pain felt, and she was glad it was gone.

She didn't want the pain anymore. She wondered why Michael had done such a thing to her. She'd been a good wife. One morning as Lorena brought in her breakfast she announced that Dr. Rinaldi wouldn't be in to see Jenni until later.

Shattered

"Can we go for a walk?" Jenni asked Lorena. Lorena and Dr. Rinaldi were the only two people she ever saw. She'd not been allowed to socialize with the other patients. "I am so sick of being cooped up in this room."

Lorena brushed back her frizzy red hair. "I hate to disturb Dr. Rinaldi. She's not feeling well. I'll ask her about it when I see her, and then we can go later or maybe tomorrow."

"Dr. Rinaldi told me I would be getting that privilege very soon. Didn't she tell you that?"

Lorena's curls bobbed as she agreed with Jenni. "Yes, she did, but she didn't tell me when."

"How could one little walk hurt?"

Lorena frowned. She didn't think it could hurt, but she hated to do anything without direct orders from Dr. Rinaldi, especially with Mrs. Hamilton. Dr. Rinaldi had been so hush-hush about her treatment and very specific about being the one to oversee all aspects of her treatment, even fixing her food trays herself.

Lorena had already taken it on herself that morning to give Mrs. Hamilton breakfast without waiting for Dr. Rinaldi. Lorena hated to let her take a walk without permission, but she didn't understand why Mrs. Hamilton wasn't allowed out of her room like the other clients. Walking and exercise were good for people suffering from depression. Being stuck in a room all alone day after day wasn't the usual treatment for depression.

Chapter Seven

She relented. "I suppose one short walk wouldn't hurt. You're not going to try and run away, are you? I need my job."

Jenni shook her head. "I wouldn't do that. I promise."

"Just don't mention it to Dr. Rinaldi. She hates for me to do things she hasn't specifically ordered. I'll be back in a few minutes to take you."

Jenni could barely contain her excitement when Lorena came back for her. They walked down a hall and out the back way. Lorena opened the door with a nervous glance at Jenni. She didn't want to lose her job over this.

Jenni smiled with the excitement of a child. "Don't worry. I promised I wouldn't run away." She walked out into the glaring sunshine. Her eyes protested at the brightness but soon adjusted. Jenni took a deep breath of fresh air. It smelled like grass. The sun warmed her skin. Jenni was amazed at how wonderful the simple act of going outside had become. Her world had grown so small since Michael. . . . She pushed the thought of his name away. She didn't like to think of Michael anymore. There wasn't any point to it.

They walked in silence, and Jenni felt how tight her muscles had grown. She promised herself to begin an exercise regime that very day. After a few minutes, Lorena insisted they go back inside. Jenni wanted to protest but knew that would be ungracious.

Shattered

Once back in the room, Jenni performed a series of calisthenics and then ran in place for several minutes. She tired easily and her heart raced from the exertion, but she forced herself to continue. After fifteen minutes, she collapsed on the bed but promised herself that she would have another session later in the day.

She walked over to the bookshelf. She'd read most of the books. She looked at the book of poetry. Jenni had avoided that book knowing it would be filled with poems of love, but it was the only book left on the shelf that she hadn't read.

She thumbed through the pages, glancing at the poems. Her eyes stopped. Her heart raced and tears sprang to her eyes. She felt off balance. Jenni read the words. Pictures flashed in her mind.

It was her wedding day. Michael and Jenni had each picked a poem to read during the ceremony. She tried to shut out the memories but couldn't. She looked at the page. Her heart fluttered as she read the words. The words blurred as tears formed.

> I love you.
> Once I told you I didn't want to hear those words.
> Once I told you those words meant nothing.
> Once I told you those words held only lies and empty promises.
>
> But you just smiled gently.
> But you just acted kindly.

Chapter Seven

But you just listened patiently.

Then you made me laugh again.
Then you made me hope again.
Then you made me trust again.

And now I understand the promise behind those words.
And now I understand the commitment behind those words.
And now I believe those words when I hear you say them.

So as I stand here today in front of our friends,
Our families,
And in front of our God, let me say,
I Love You.

No one knows the future.
No one knows what obstacles lie ahead.
No one knows what wonderful adventures lie ahead.

But this I do know,
From this day forth, we will walk together hand in hand
To discover what God has planned.

I love you, today, tomorrow, and forever.

"Oh, Michael, how could you do this to me? Why did you leave me?"

Shattered

A sob burst forth and she dropped the book and rushed into the bathroom. She reached for the bath oils, the soft soothing oils, but changed her mind and jumped into the shower instead.

She turned the water from hot to cold and let the icy needles wash away the cobwebs in her mind. Tears mingled with the shower water. The pictures kept flashing. She was in her wedding dress. Michael—smiling as she walked down the aisle. Michael—slipping the ring on her finger. Michael—holding her the day she knew she would never have a child. She felt emotions churning inside her. She tried to push them away.

She saw herself reading the poem to Michael. She'd chosen it because it had expressed what she'd felt perfectly. She had never trusted anyone until Michael. He had taught her how to trust and how to love and now it had all been ripped from her.

The cold water sprayed against her skin, forcing her to feel it. She shook her head. She didn't want the feelings anymore. Michael was gone. He had broken their marriage vows. He had betrayed her. He had broken his promise. She had to make a new life for herself without him. She sobbed. She turned the water back to hot.

Another picture of Michael came to mind: he was walking out the door the day he died; he turned to her and said, "I love you, sweetie pie." For a moment, she couldn't catch her breath, and then she whispered, "I love you too, Michael."

Chapter Seven

With those words, the dam of emotions broke. She slid down to the tub and moaned. The pain was so strong that she could feel it throughout her body. She trembled even though the water was steaming hot.

When the sobs subsided, she turned off the shower water. She shivered. She looked at herself in the mirror. It was as if she were awake for the first time in a long time. She was confused. When she'd first come here, she'd believed in Michael and their vows but somewhere along the way she'd forgotten that. She'd started believing in the lies again. She'd forgotten that Michael loved her. She wrapped herself in a towel and then used a second towel as a turban for her wet hair.

She moved into the other room. The book lay on the floor. She picked it up and cradled it in her arms. She read the poem again. Her eyes filled with tears, but this time it was happy tears.

Her hand went to the juice, but she stopped as the glass met her lips. She looked at the glass thoughtfully. Lorena always brought juice in shortly before her sessions with Dr. Rinaldi.

She'd known from the beginning that she was probably being drugged, but somewhere along the way she'd stopped worrying about it. She picked up the glass and went to the bathroom. She poured it down the sink.

She went back to the chair and closed her eyes trying to quiet the thoughts and feelings that raced inside

Shattered

her. Jenni opened her eyes as the door opened but closed them again before Dr. Rinaldi looked at her.

Gail Rinaldi saw a sleeping woman holding a book of poetry. She glanced at the empty glass of juice smiled. *Things are going well indeed.* She walked over to Jenni. She took the book from Jenni's hands and gave her a soft shake. Jenni prayed that she could look calm even though she was feeling completely out of control. Jenni opened her eyes and smiled peacefully.

Dr. Rinaldi began speaking in that same soothing voice she always used. Jenni closed her eyes. Jenni focused on the words. "You are such a good person, Jenni. Michael didn't deserve your love." *That's not true.* "He's gone and now you have the opportunity to be really happy. He didn't make you happy. He never made you happy." *Yes, he did,* Jenni's mind screamed, but she forced the peaceful smile. "When it's time to leave here, you will forget all about trying to find the truth. You know the truth. He stole money, he betrayed you with another woman, he was arrested, and then he killed himself. That is the truth."

The voice droned on, and Jenni's body relaxed as she listened, but she fought against it. She knew the words were lies. She knew Michael hadn't killed himself. No matter what else he did or didn't do. Michael was a Christian, and he would never have killed himself. She struggled not to listen to the words. Forcing

Chapter Seven

herself to breathe deeply and evenly, not showing the turmoil that she was feeling.

Not knowing what else to do, Jenni began praying the Lord's Prayer to herself. When she was finished, she repeated it again and again until Dr. Rinaldi left. Eventually Dr. Rinaldi left, assuming that she'd had yet another successful session with Jenni. She'd been worried since she'd been too ill that morning to make sure that Jenni received her morning meds, but there'd been no setback. That was good. She wanted this whole episode to end, but she was committed now to finishing the job she'd started.

Jenni kept her eyes closed for a long time after Dr. Rinaldi left.

She finally opened her eyes and sat up in the chair. What had happened to her? Why had she been able to break through the apathy of the drugs? Then she understood; Dr. Rinaldi had not been the one to fix her breakfast that morning as she usually did. Lorena had told Jenni that Dr. Rinaldi had been sick that morning. Not only had Jenni not been drugged, but also Lorena had allowed her to go outside to exercise and get fresh air. *Thank you, Lorena.*

The combination of no drugs that morning plus the physical exercise had been enough to clear her mind enough that she could think for herself for the first time in a long time. Jenni knew that it would be a struggle each day. She didn't have the strength to do it alone.

Shattered

She fell to her knees and began praying for strength to fight the evil being done to her.

When she finished praying, Jenni picked up the book of poetry but didn't open it. She just held it. *I won't let them win, Michael. I will find out who did this to you.* She didn't know how she would manage it, but she wouldn't let them brainwash her into believing the horrible lies they were saying about Michael. She would have to fight them.

She stood and began jogging in place. *Let me think about Michael.* She let her mind think back to the first day that she'd met Michael. She'd been twenty-two at the time and working at a fast food place. He'd walked in and her life had never been the same.

Jenni shook her head. She'd been such a mess back then and hadn't even known it at the time, but being with Michael had changed all that. He'd loved her just the way she was and that gave her the courage to become a better person. It hadn't been easy. She'd resisted him and his charms, but he'd pursued her until she gave in.

It had been during a rush, and she hadn't noticed him at first, but she did notice him when he'd stayed in her line instead of jumping to a shorter line. She gave him a quick smile but forgot about him until it was his turn to be served.

"What do you want?" She had to look up to ask him. He was very tall.

"A date with you," he'd answered. His ears were red with embarrassment.

Chapter Seven

She rolled her eyes. "I don't have time for this. Tell me what you want."

"I just did."

"Cute. Now, give me your order."

He did. When she handed him the food, he asked her again, "So, how about that date?"

"I've got a boyfriend."

"I don't care."

She laughed. "You would if you saw him. It wouldn't be good for you to make him mad."

"I'm not afraid of him." He puffed up his skinny chest.

"That's nice but no thanks." She forgot about the cute, nerdy boy until the next day. They went through the whole routine again. He came the next day and the day after. After five days, she finally agreed to a date.

Three more weeks and she'd broken up with her other boyfriend.

The pain in her side brought her back to the present. She was breathing hard and sweating. She needed to get back in shape. She sat down on the bed and thought of Michael.

Chapter Eight

The next morning Lorena brought her juice and her breakfast.

"Lorena, did you make my breakfast tray up for me?" Jenni asked, trying to sound innocent.

"No, Dr. Rinaldi did. Why?"

"Oh no reason, I just remembered that you said you'd done it yesterday. I thought that maybe you were doing it now. Dr. Rinaldi must have more important things to do than fix my breakfast."

"Her patients are the most important thing to her. She is a wonderful doctor."

When she left, Jenni rushed to the bathroom and poured the juice down the sink. She carefully washed out the sink, not wanting Dr. Rinaldi to know that she'd dumped it. She could only hope that her room didn't have some kind of hidden camera in it. She hadn't no-

Shattered

ticed anything that looked like a video camera, but it was hard to know these days.

Dr. Rinaldi walked in fifteen minutes later.

"Hello, Dr. Rinaldi." Jenni smiled pleasantly at the woman. "I wanted to know if I could get a Bible to read."

Dr. Rinaldi studied Jenni as she thought about it. She finally spoke. "I didn't know you were religious."

"I am. I miss going to church. I haven't been there since Michael died." She managed to keep her voice on an even keel as she talked.

"I don't see why not. Speaking of the Bible, I wonder how many commandments Michael broke."

Jenni felt the urge to slap this woman. How dare she use the Bible in her evil plan. Instead, Jenni leaned back and closed her eyes. Dr. Rinaldi began to speak. Jenni thought back to the day Michael had asked her to marry him.

They'd spent the summer camping out before marriage and following Bruce Springsteen around the country. This would be the last concert and then it would be back to school for Michael and Jenni would need to find a job. She'd quit hers so she could spend the summer with Michael.

They'd gone on a picnic. It had been a beautiful day, but the sun was setting. He'd suggested a walk to the lake before they left. The water shimmered with the colors of the setting sun. The geese surrounded them

Chapter Eight

for breadcrumbs. When the bread was gone, the geese lost interest in Jenni and Michael and waddled away.

They sat down on a bench.

"Did you know that geese mate for life?"

"Well, they're probably the only ones."

They'd discussed the idea of marriage many times, and Jenni had made her views quite clear. She didn't believe that men could stay faithful. Her father had proven that when he'd left her and her mother years before.

"That's not true, Jenni. Lots of people get married and stay married."

"Not any more."

"Look at my parents."

"Yeah, but your parents are perfect. I come from bad genes. Marriage isn't good for the women in my family."

"I don't believe that." That's when he got down on his knees and pulled out the ring. After he'd asked her, she couldn't speak. He assumed that was because her answer would be no, but the truth was she couldn't speak because she was afraid that she would cry.

"I know you're afraid of marriage, but I promise we'll be like the geese. We'll be married for life. I promise to love you and cherish you and to take care of you."

She finally found her voice. "OK, but I'm going to hold you to that promise."

Dr. Rinaldi stopped talking, and Jenni waited to hear the door close. She sat up wiping away the tears that she couldn't stop from falling.

Shattered

Lorena brought in a Bible later that day, and Jenni began reading it avidly. She would alternate between reading, praying, and exercising. For the next several days, she did her best to act as if she were still being drugged. When Dr. Rinaldi would begin to speak, Jenni would begin singing old hymns to herself or praying. She knew she couldn't get out of that clinic alone. She needed God's help.

After several more days, their sessions changed. Dr. Rinaldi began to expect her to participate in the sessions. Jenni worked hard to give the performance of a lifetime, and as far as Jenni was concerned, she was worthy of an Oscar.

Her food and juice would be waiting for her after she showered each day. She would dump the juice down the drain and eat only a minimum amount of food. She exercised several times each day and spent much time thinking about Michael and their life together.

During her sessions with Dr. Rinaldi, Jenni smiled a lot and told Dr. Rinaldi the things she thought Dr. Rinaldi wanted to hear. She would agree that Michael hadn't deserved her love, but inside she would be screaming the truth. Then came the day when Dr. Rinaldi encouraged Jenni to begin making plans for the future. Jenni knew she'd won the battle.

With Dr. Rinaldi's approval, Jenni made travel arrangements to visit a cousin in California. She told Dr. Rinaldi that she wanted to get far away from all

Chapter Eight

the memories of Michael. She was even thinking of moving there if she liked the area. Her mother packed suitcases for Jenni so she wouldn't have to go home. No need for bad memories. Jenni had smiled and agreed with Dr. Rinaldi.

But Jenni made her own plans. She had no intention of going to California. They, whoever they were, didn't want her going to the Bahamas, and so that was exactly where Jenni was going, but she needed her passport. She was afraid Dr. Rinaldi would be suspicious if she asked her mother to pack it.

The day before she was to leave, she was talking to Dr. Rinaldi.

"Is it OK if I make a phone call?"

"Sure, who do you need to call?"

"I wanted to call Carmen and tell her to meet me at the airport before I leave. I wanted her to see with her own eyes that I am OK, now. I don't want her to have to worry about me the whole time I'm gone."

"That's very thoughtful of you, but do you think it will upset you to see her?"

Jenni looked directly into Dr. Rinaldi's eyes to show that she wasn't feeling any anxiety. "Not at all, we've been friends for a long time. Our friendship was more than just a friendship between wives. I'm sure she will want to see me before I go."

Shattered

Dr. Rinaldi walked Jenni to her own office and got busy with paperwork as Jenni made her call. She listened discretely to Jenni's side of the conversation.

I'm fine, Carmen.

I'm better than I have been in months.

No, I don't want to talk about Michael. That part of my life is over.

I'm going to go spend time with my cousin.
Can you come and see me at the airport before I leave?

I forgot to have my mom pick up my trip journal. You know the one that I wanted to take with us on the trip to Mexico and I forgot it then, too? You know, that time we had all that trouble at the border crossing and we had to wait an extra day?

Yes, that's the book I want. I'll be at the airport tomorrow morning at eleven.

See you then.

Jenni turned back to Dr. Rinaldi and smiled.
"I didn't forget to tell my mother about the journal. I knew if she saw it she would read it, and my journal is private."

Chapter Eight

"Mothers can be that way, can't they?" The look on Dr. Rinaldi's face turned serious. "Sometimes clients lose track of time when they're visiting us, so I just wanted to tell you the date so you won't be shocked tomorrow."

Jenni was indeed shocked when Dr. Rinaldi told her that more than seven weeks had gone by while she had been locked up in the clinic. Jenni had thought she'd been there only a few weeks.

Chapter Nine

Beth Collins was tapping her foot and smoking a cigarette when Jenni walked into Dr. Rinaldi's office. They hadn't seen each other since Jenni had been hospitalized. She knew Jenni hated her, but she'd had no choice. Mr. Peyton, Miss Meyers, even Roberto had felt that Jenni was becoming a danger to herself. A mother's first job is always to protect her child, no matter how difficult.

Instead, Jenni walked in and hugged her mom. It took a moment but then Beth hugged her back. Her mother's shoulders relaxed. Jenni truly wasn't mad at her mom. That wasn't an act. Jenni believed that her mother was as much a victim as Jenni. She was only trying to help Jenni. It wasn't her fault that she was being used in some game that neither of them understood but Jenni had every intention of finding out.

Shattered

Her mother started crying. "I'm so sorry, Jenni. I didn't want to do it, but I had to do something to help you."

Jenni hugged her mother even closer. "It's OK, Mama. I know you were just trying to help, and you did help me. Thank you."

Her mother stepped back and wiped the tears. She asked, "You're not mad at me?"

"No, Mama. I'm not mad. You did what you needed to do. I'm much better now."

As they were leaving, Dr. Rinaldi handed Jenni her business card. Jenni smiled sweetly at her even though she really wanted to throw the card back in her face.

They were on the way to the airport and her mom was driving. Jenni spoke softly. "Mom, I want to thank you for helping me. I know it must have been a difficult decision."

Her mother swerved as she turned to look at Jenni. "I hated doing it. I might not have done it, but Roberto assured me that it was the right thing to do."

Jenni felt the sting of betrayal as if someone had slapped her at the mention of Roberto. It was hard for her to believe that Roberto would ever hurt Michael or herself but why would he have had her committed if that weren't the case. She refused to let her mother see that she'd been upset by her words. Her plan to get to the Bahamas would only work as long as everyone believed she was going to California.

Chapter Nine

"You were just trying to help me." She patted her mom's shoulder. Jenni kept her voice calm as she asked, "Who else helped you?"

"Mr. Peyton went with us. He paid for your hospital stay, or at least what your insurance wouldn't cover."

Jenni's mind was racing. Roberto and Nicholas Peyton knew each other through Michael. Were they in this conspiracy together? She would never have believed that Roberto would ever do anything to hurt Michael, but the facts spoke for themselves. She thought about it for a few moments, but discarded the idea. Roberto must be a pawn much the same as her mother.

Her mother looked at her sharply. "Are you OK? What's wrong?"

"Nothing."

"You seem angry. Maybe we should call Dr. Rinaldi."

Heaven forbid that her mother do that. Jenni fought to regain control of her emotions. "I'm fine. Don't be such a worry wart." She patted her mother just to prove how all right she was.

"Maybe she let you out too soon."

"Not soon enough as far as I'm concerned."

Another sharp look and a bit of a swerve with the car.

"I'm just teasing you, Ma. I needed time to get my head straight." Her mother smiled but still looked doubtful.

They pulled up to the drop-off lane at the airport. Carmen was pacing back and forth, her long hair sway-

Shattered

ing with each turn. "Look. There's Carmen, she'll help me with the luggage, Mom." Jenni gave her mom a big hug meant to reassure her.

"I'll park and then I'll be right in."

"That's OK. I'll just wait with Carmen until my plane leaves. We have a lot of gossip to catch up on."

"But I promised Dr. Rinaldi that I would stay with you."

I'll just bet you did. "I'm fine. Carmen will stay with me. I'll call you tomorrow."

Her mother looked uncertain but nodded. As Jenni pulled her luggage out of the trunk, Carmen spotted her and rushed toward her. They were hugging and crying as Beth Collins drove off with a backward glance in the mirror. Jenni did not seem as OK as the doctor had said. Perhaps she should call the doctor. She began to look for a pay phone.

Chapter Ten

Gail Rinaldi closed the cell phone harder than necessary. Her lover stared at her.

"Is there a problem?"

"I'm not sure. That was Beth Collins. She said that Jenni was acting strangely on the way to the airport."

"Acting strange, how?"

"Angry, and then she wouldn't let her mother go in the airport with her." Gail tapped the phone with her nails.

"Well, that shouldn't be surprising. Her mother did have her committed to the hospital against her wishes."

"She shouldn't be angry. During the hypnosis, I helped her deal with the anger."

"What are you saying? That the hypnosis didn't work?"

Gail didn't want to make her lover angry, so she tried to soft pedal around that issue. "I'm not saying that. I'm just saying it doesn't make sense."

Shattered

"So, what are you going to do?"

"Her plane doesn't leave for another hour and a half. I think I'll go out there and talk to her. Just to make sure."

"You promised you could take care of this. I told you I could take care of it another way, but you promised this would work."

"And I'm sure it did, sweetheart. I just want to go talk to her for my own peace of mind."

"Call me if there's a problem at the airport. I have to make sure she won't cause a problem. My father is counting on me to take care of this."

Gail left their rendezvous apartment and drove to the airport wondering how she'd ever gotten involved in this mess. She'd never done anything that could be considered illegal or unethical, and yet she'd done both for the sake of love. She shook her head disgusted with herself.

It wasn't worth it.

Chapter Eleven

Jenni and Carmen were sitting at a fast food restaurant at the airport. Jenni sipped on her soda, then asked Carmen, "Did you tell Roberto you were meeting me and bringing me my passport?" She tried to make her voice casual.

Carmen gave her an odd look but said in a quiet voice, "No."

Both chose not to pursue that topic for their own reasons. Jenni knew Carmen would have to be told about Roberto and his actions, but now wasn't the right time.

Carmen changed the subject. "So, what happened at the hospital?"

Jenni told her a short version of her stay in the clinic as they waited in line to exchange her ticket. "Carmen, I know that God protected me while I was there. I couldn't have resisted the hypnosis or the drugs without his help. I know he protected me."

"Of course, God keeps his promises."

"I was really mad at God after Michael died. I blamed it on him, but now I understand that it was evilness that killed Michael, not God. Michael told me time after time that we all have to fight against evil whenever we encounter it, and so that's what I'm trying to do."

"You are amazing, Jenni. What are you going to do now?"

"What I was going to do before they kidnapped me. I'm going to the Bahamas and talk to Jasmine DuPree. If Michael were going to leave me and go be with her, I want to know it, and I'm not going to believe it until she proves it to me."

Carmen nodded in agreement. "That's what I figured when you called and told me to get your passport, so I looked through Roberto's files and got her name and address for you." Carmen handed her a paper.

After she'd exchanged tickets and gotten everything straightened out, Jenni excused herself to go to the restroom. Carmen said she would pop into a few of the shops while she waited.

When Jenni went to find Carmen, she turned a corner that led back toward the restaurant. She saw Carmen talking with someone. As she got closer, Jenni recognized her mother and Dr. Rinaldi. Carmen's eyes met Jenni's, and even from that distance, Jenni recognized the panic in them

Chapter Eleven

What is wrong with my mother? She just keeps doing the wrong thing. Jenni turned back toward the ladies room but realized that was stupid. It would be the first place they would look.

She heard her name being called over the loudspeaker. She was being paged. She walked past a beauty shop. *Who would take the time to have their hair done at the airport?* She kept walking but then stopped. Two hours later, Jenni walked out of the salon. Her long brown hair was now short and the deep rich red of Bing cherries just before they turned dark.

She didn't know if it looked good, but it looked different. She had missed her plane to the Bahamas, which wasn't that big of a deal since she probably wouldn't have been allowed to board anyway. No doubt Dr. Rinaldi and her mother had worked up some scheme to take her back to the clinic.

She hoped it was safe for her to go back to the ticket counter and exchange the ticket for another destination, anywhere, as long as she got out of town. She could get another plane to the Bahamas from somewhere else. For now, she just needed to get away from her mother and Dr. Rinaldi.

She knew the answer soon enough. Amazingly enough, not only did she find her mother's face in the sea of people, but a police officer was standing with her. They were searching the crowd looking for her.

Shattered

She went to the first gift shop she saw. She bought an extra large T-shirt and a baseball cap. She immediately slipped them over her own clothes. She affected the angry walk of a teenager. She kept her head down and made a beeline for the luggage area so she could get a cab without a problem. The only problem was Dr. Rinaldi was standing in front of that door with another officer.

Jenni made a sharp U-turn and found an escalator. She stepped on it. She followed the sea of people and walked out of a door with them. She ended up in long-term parking. Oh, well. She began walking.

It was a hot day and two layers of clothes made it even worse. She trekked up the ramp and saw a cab drop off a couple. She dashed toward it. He held the door open for her, and she slid into the welcomed coolness of the air-conditioned car.

She gave the driver her address and sat back trying to calm down. They turned down her street. A police car sat in her driveway. She thanked her lucky stars that Michael had never gotten around to putting up those privacy bushes she had begged for year after year.

"Stop!" she screamed at the driver.

He slowed down but didn't stop. "What's wrong?"

How could she explain this without seeming like an idiot? She started to lie but stopped. "I saw a police car at my house, and I'd rather not deal with them right now."

Chapter Eleven

He made a left turn away from her house. Then looked at her with suspicion. "Are you in trouble, 'cause I don't want no trouble."

"Not really. My mother doesn't like the travel plans, so she called my doctor. They want to put me in the hospital."

"So, do the cops want to arrest you?"

"No, just put me in the hospital."

"Why?"

"My husband died a few months ago, and everyone wants me to pretend like it didn't matter. As if it's not normal to grieve for your husband of twenty years."

The cabbie's voice softened and he nodded vigorously. "I know. I lost my Lydia three years ago, and everyone keeps saying 'replace her, replace her,' like I could."

"Then you know what I mean."

"I certainly do, lady. Where do you want to go?"

Where did she want to go? "How about the bus station?"

As she was leaving she told the cabbie, "I'm sorry you lost your wife."

He looked confused.

"Lydia, your wife."

He shook his head. "My wife. No, no. Lydia was my beagle, but she was the best beagle in the world."

Jenni forced herself not to smile. "Thanks so much for trusting me."

Shattered

"Not a problem, lady. Good luck with that mother of yours. She sounds like a pistol."

Jenni walked into the bus station; she felt completely alone. All she had with her was her purse and passport, but that was all she needed.

Chapter Twelve

The tropical heat engulfed her as Jenni disembarked from the plane. She saw the cloudless blue sky and palm trees lining the walkway. It had been a long time since she'd been there. It was hard to breathe, but she wasn't sure if it was from the heat or the memories.

She brushed the memories away and focused on the present. She bit her lip as she thought of the task that lay ahead. She was filled with confusion. She had convinced herself that Michael would absolutely not do the things they said, but a small part of her thought of all the evidence she'd seen. She knew a part of her believed that it all might be true. That was why she was in the Bahamas. She needed to know. She couldn't let go of the past until she knew if Michael's love had been real.

Still feeling jittery and paranoid, she looked around the airport. It wouldn't have surprised her to see Dr. Rinaldi and her mother waiting for her, but she didn't.

Shattered

She sighed with relief. At least she didn't have to worry about them for now.

She stood in line waiting for customs. She had a small carry-on that she'd purchased in Pittsburgh. That was where the first bus was going, so she'd bought a ticket. Her turn came and in minutes she was free to go. She walked across the tiny airport that was filled with people enjoying the tropical paradise. She went to the next cab waiting in line.

The driver hopped out and opened the door for her.

"Where to?"

"I was hoping you could help me with that. I don't have reservations, but I want to go to a small hotel, not these big ones around here."

"Not a problem. I know the perfect one, right by the beach."

He drove her to an older hotel that had seen better days. Jenni sat on the bed fingering the paper with the address of Jasmine DuPree. The ceiling fan moved the hot air around the room making the heat bearable, but just barely. The room was old and had what the travel agents would call character, not like the cookie-cutter rooms in the big resort hotels but of course those rooms had air conditioning.

She stared at the worn paper in her hand. Tomorrow would be soon enough. She sat on the patio with her face lifted to the sun. The warm ocean breeze caressed her. She smelled the saltiness in the air. Emotions

Chapter Twelve

bubbled up as memories came back. Michael had brought her to the Bahamas several times before he came here alone; they'd never come back after that.

The first time had been about two years after they were married; they called it their honeymoon since they couldn't afford to go on one when they'd gotten married. All their money went to pay Michael's tuition. He'd been lucky to get a job immediately after college, but unbeknownst to her, he had talked his employers into an advance. He'd used that advance to book them on a long weekend to the Bahamas.

They'd gone on one of those gambling packages to the big resort on the island, but they'd spent less than a half-hour in the casino. Their days had been spent lounging in the hot sun on the beach that the hotel had shuttled them to, and their evenings had been spent on long walks in the moonlight talking about their plans for the future. It had only been three nights and probably one of the cheapest trips they'd ever gone on, but it had been the most romantic trip of their marriage.

She tasted the saltiness of the ocean on her tongue but then realized it was tears. She went into the room and flung herself on the bed and sobbed. She was barely surviving without Michael, but she knew she couldn't survive his betrayal. She was beginning to regret even coming. Maybe Dr. Rinaldi was right all along, maybe she should just leave well enough alone and get on with her life.

Shattered

The pain was so intense that it was physical; she felt her heart breaking. She curled up in a fetal position wishing all of this would go away. She prayed for calmness. When the tears finally passed, she knew she would go see Jasmine DuPree the next day. She couldn't leave without knowing the truth, no matter how much it hurt. She had to know.

She took a shower and dressed for dinner. She wasn't really hungry, but she needed to get out of that room. She put on one of the new dresses that she'd bought at the Pittsburgh airport. It was a sundress with a tropical flavor; just the kind of thing you'd never wear at home but always seemed perfect on vacation.

She ran her fingers through her new red hairdo to fluff it and was surprised at her image in the mirror. She saw a rather stunning woman staring back at her. She didn't look like the middle-aged, brokenhearted widow that she was.

She walked to the hotel restaurant. It was more than adequate for a meal. She wasn't in the mood for sightseeing. The restaurant sported ceiling fans just as her room did, but Jenni detected a hint of air conditioning. There was absolutely no ambiance; it looked like any of a hundred small diners that could be found in any town across America.

She chose a table in the corner and looked at the menu. She chose the conch chowder. *Michael had loved that chowder.* She pushed the thought away; she refused

Chapter Twelve

to get mired down in memories. There was no way she would get through the next few days if she kept thinking that way. She looked around her; most of the tables were empty, but the counter was crowded.

One man turned and smiled at her. His brown hair was pulled back in a ponytail, and he was wearing shorts and sandals. Jenni resisted the urge tell the man that it was time to grow up and give up the ponytail; the '60s had been over for a long time. He gave her a wink and she turned away. Her pulse quickened and her first thought was to flee, but knew she was being ridiculous. She told herself to stop being so paranoid.

"Excuse me." She looked up. A man stood above her smiling down. He was about Jenni's age and appeared to be a businessman. He had a jagged scar under his eye. She wondered how that had happened. "Hi, I thought you might like to have a drink with me."

"No thanks."

"Then, how about a walk after dinner?"

"No thanks."

"You don't want to spend a beautiful evening like this alone, do you?"

"Actually, I do." She turned away. He looked disappointed and went to another table. When she was finished eating, she paid the bill and walked out. She'd only taken a few steps when she heard a voice.

"Excuse me." She turned. The businessman was a few steps behind her. "Are you ready for that walk?"

Shattered

She moved back a few steps alarmed at his closeness. "I told you no."

"I know, but you're just too beautiful to be alone tonight." He stepped toward her and put an arm on her elbow. She smelled the alcohol. "We can take a walk on the beach and star gaze."

Jenni jerked away but he didn't let go of her elbow. Her voice turned shrill. "I already told you no. Leave me alone." He stepped in closer and tightened his grip. She pushed at him, but his fingers pressed into her flesh causing her to wince in pain. He pulled her toward the beach. She struggled.

"Leave her alone," a voice called out from the darkness.

"You leave us alone." He dragged her further down the path. "It's none of your business."

A man came out of the shadows and was by her side. "Let go of her." And to emphasize his point, he grabbed her assailant from behind and threw him to the ground. The drunk stayed on the ground.

"Do you want me to call the police?" asked the man. Jenny recognized him as the man with the ponytail from the restaurant.

Jenny was quick to shake her head. "No, no. I'm fine."

He kicked the man still lying on the ground. "I'll walk you back to your room."

"Thanks." They walked away from her assailant who still lay on the ground. "I don't know what would have

Chapter Twelve

happened if you hadn't helped me." Her voice was shaky. She shuddered as the realization hit her of what could have happened.

"Are you OK?" His voice was filled with concern.

"Just an after-reaction." She looked at her rescuer. He skin was bronzed to a dark tan, and his ponytail had streaks of blonde mixed in with the brown. He looked to be a middle-aged surf bum. His jean shorts were much too short and tight for a man his age, which only added to the picture of a man that didn't want to grow up.

He held out his hand. "I'm Billy Bob." She detected a hint of a southern accent.

"I'm . . . Caroline." She didn't want him to know her name.

"You don't look like a Caroline."

She shrugged.

"No, you look more like a . . ." She tensed, positive that he was going to say her name. "Well, I don't know, but not a Caroline."

She relaxed and let out her breath, not realizing she had been holding it.

"So what are you doing here?" Billy Bob asked.

"Eating dinner."

He shook his head and smiled. "No, I mean what are you doing in the Bahamas?"

"Just a little business. What about you?" Jenni changed the subject. She didn't want to answer his questions.

"Just here for the diving."

Jenni smiled. She'd almost been right—diving, not surfing. He probably worked some menial job, saved all his money, and went from beach to beach. Not a bad life if you didn't have any family responsibilities.

"I can't thank you enough for helping me."

He smiled slowly. His southern accent more pronounced. "Sure you can, just have a drink with me."

"Oh, I can't," she responded quickly.

He looked taken aback by her abruptness. "Oh, that's OK. No problem. I'm sure after that you just want to be alone."

Billy Bob walked Jenni back to her room. He'd insisted. At the door, she fumbled in her purse to find the room key. She fished it out and held it up to show off her trophy. Billy Bob smiled at her accomplishment. His hand moved up to her face and brushed away a hair. She was startled by his touch and stepped back.

"Sorry. I didn't mean to scare you."

She smiled back and shook her head. "That's OK. It's just—"

"I know. I saw the ring. Can we have dinner together tomorrow night? Nothing special, just two people eating dinner. It's better than eating alone."

She smiled. "I'm not sure. I have to do something difficult tomorrow, and I'm not sure how I'll be feeling. Give me your room number, and I'll either call or leave a message for you at the desk sometime in the afternoon."

Chapter Twelve

"Anything I can do to help, ma'am?" He drawled in his best cowboy accent.

She shook her head. "No, this is something I have to do alone."

They said their good-byes, and he left her alone.

Chapter Thirteen

When Jenni awoke the next morning, the heat had already invaded the room. She spent a long time on her knees in prayer. She couldn't face the day alone. She finally stood up, calm and resolved. She took a cool shower and dressed. She didn't know what the day would bring but she was ready. The split-skirt combo that she put on was an olive green and made her red hair more vibrant in the bright sunshine of the tropical day.

She ordered room service, not wanting to see anyone. Finally she couldn't put it off any longer, so she went outside to find a taxi. She told herself the heat was the reason her chest was tight and her breathing was labored.

She had been telling herself that she was doing this for Michael, but now she knew that wasn't true. She was doing it for herself. She needed to know if the man she'd loved and had known for more than half her life

Shattered

had been an illusion. She needed to know if their love had been real. She needed to know if Michael had been real. Either way, she would now be able to face it with God's help, but she wanted to know the truth.

The taxi drove her to what looked like a middle-class neighborhood. The lawns were small but neatly trimmed and lush with a multitude of tropical plants and flowers. The houses were stucco, in a rainbow of colors. Children played and screamed in the yards, but not in the one the driver pulled up to.

She paid the cab driver and watched him drive away. She took a deep breath and walked resolutely up to the steps noticing that this house looked no different from any of the others on the block, and yet it was different. Supposedly, her husband stole money to buy this house, or so the authorities would have her believe.

She lost count of the number of times she rang the bell before she admitted that no one was home. She should have asked the taxi to wait.

A neighbor's head poked out an upstairs window. "Hello. She's not home." The woman spoke in the lilting way of the islanders.

"Do you know when she will be back?"

"Not until late. She works at the restaurant until it closes."

"Do you know what restaurant she works at?"

"No, no, she don't just work at the restaurant, she owns it." This was said in a tone that was meant to convey the fact that Jasmine was no ordinary waitress.

Chapter Thirteen

"She does?"

"Oh, my yes. She's so proud of that restaurant. She works hard for her restaurant."

Jenni felt tightening in her chest. She didn't want to ask the next question. "Has she owned it long?"

"No, no. Just about six months, the same time when she moved in here."

Jenni felt a lump in her stomach. It didn't take much imagination to figure out where she had gotten the money.

"What's the name of it?"

"Tropical Breezes. It is a beautiful restaurant, and the food is delicious, not some of the swill like in those tourist restaurants."

"Can I call a taxi from your house to take me there?"

"No need, no need. It's not far at all, you can walk there."

After forty-five minutes of walking in the blistering heat, Jenni began to wonder what the woman meant by not far, obviously not the same as her definition. Jenni spied a restaurant and decided to take a break. She walked gratefully into the air-conditioned building and found a table. Her hair was soaked in sweat and pasted to her head and likewise so were her clothes. At least her feet didn't hurt; she was glad she'd kept her old comfortable running shoes on that morning even if they looked silly with her outfit.

Shattered

The waitress came with a glass of water that Jenni gulped down before ordering a large glass of lemonade to help her cool off before she went into Tropical Breezes. She didn't even mind that there was so little sugar in that her mouth puckered as she drank it.

She took several deep breaths and tried to clear her mind for the difficult task that was facing her. She'd never thought she would have to meet the woman that Michael had been unfaithful with. After all, they lived in different countries; there was no reason for their paths to ever cross. After that affair, the subject of visiting the Bahamas never came up. They always had other places to choose from, but here she sat, preparing to meet the woman.

Over the years, Jenni had heard so many women say that they would never forgive their husbands if he had an affair. That they would leave in a heartbeat. She'd even been one of those women, but it wasn't so easy to throw away a lifetime of work and memories for a mistake, a big mistake, but still a mistake.

A marriage was made up of so much more than sex. It seemed wrong somehow to throw it all away because of sex. At least that's what she told herself, not knowing whether it was a rationalization or the truth.

She took one deep breath, stood up, paid the bill, and left to go find Tropical Breezes, which according to the waitress, was only a block away. She didn't think about what she might find out. She walked resolutely up to the door, no hesitation, and no second thoughts.

Chapter Thirteen

She walked through the door and looked around her. The restaurant had a tropical rainforest theme going; tropical plants abounded, and all the walls had been painted with animals from the rain forest. The tables were empty.

A woman called from the back, "We are not open yet, but sit wherever you like, I'll be out in a minute."

Jenni did not sit down. She remained standing in the middle of the restaurant. A few moments later a woman stepped in the room. Her beauty surprised Jenni. She was tall, and the strapless sundress she wore showed off her statuesque body. Her skin was the color of mocha latte, and her hair was a soft brown with curls that flowed down her back in a ponytail.

She carried a tray. "Sit wherever you like."

Jenni tried to speak but couldn't find her voice. She stood there staring at the woman. The woman's eyes fluttered nervously, and she looked down at the floor, almost appearing to look apologetic. Jenni knew it was just an illusion since the woman couldn't possibly know who Jenni was.

"I'm looking for Jasmine DuPree."

Again the eyes fluttered. "I am Jasmine. Can I help you?"

Jenni cleared her throat nervously. "My name is Jenni Hamilton; Michael Hamilton was my husband." Jenni waited for a reaction but was disappointed there was none. Jasmine simply looked back at her.

Shattered

"I don't know if you remember Michael. He—"

"Yes, of course I know Michael." The woman's voice had taken on a hint of anger.

"He was my husband."

"Was—he divorced you." Jenni thought she detected a flicker of satisfaction, but then it disappeared.

"No, he didn't divorce me. He's dead."

The woman's face crumpled, and in spite of herself, Jenni felt a stab of pain for the woman. The tray clattered to the floor, and Jasmine slid into the nearest chair. She motioned for Jenni to sit, which Jenni did. "What do you mean dead? I don't understand. He was supposed to—" The woman stopped. "What happened? How did he die?"

"I'm here to ask questions, not answer questions. You have no right to ask me questions." Jenni's words sounded ugly, but she suddenly was overwhelmed with anger. Anger at this woman, anger at her dead husband, anger at the world.

Long moments went by. Neither of them spoke as they both worked to control her own emotions. Jasmine sat in the chair, dabbing her eyes with a napkin from the place setting on the table. Jenni broke the silence. She spoke quietly fighting back the emotions. "He died a little more than three months ago. I'm here to find out what you know about it."

"Know about it? I didn't even know he was dead. I . . . I . . . I . . ." Jasmine appeared to be at a loss for words.

Chapter Thirteen

Jenni took a calming breath. "Before he died, he was arrested for stealing money from his company. They say he bought a house here—the house you're living in—and he sent a lot of money here. I want to know what was going on."

Jasmine's eyes fluttered, and she looked up at the ceiling. She seemed to make a decision. Her face took on a look of determination, and she looked back at Jenni. "He was going to move here and take care of me, take care of us."

Before Jenni could recover her voice, a small boy ran out from the kitchen. He ran to Jasmine. He turned to face Jenni. An involuntary gasp escaped from her. She was looking into Michael's face, younger and darker, but still it was Michael's face. She couldn't breathe. She felt the oxygen escape her body. Dizziness overtook her.

The pieces of the puzzle clicked into place. This would be the only reason why Michael might do the things they'd said. It was the one thing she could never provide him, a child. She knew he would not abandon his child, he would steal, lie, and break her heart if he had to. He would do all of those things and more to take care of his child.

Jasmine hugged the boy to her hoping to protect him. Jasmine looked sad. She spoke softly. "Now you understand. I can see it in your face. He wanted to take care of us. I don't mean to cause you any more pain. He felt awful about all of it. He still loved you, but he wanted to be with us."

Shattered

Jenni struggled to control her emotions.

"He kept in touch with you all those years."

"Yes, of course."

"And you've been seeing him all along?"

"Not much. Sometimes we would fly to New York to meet, but then he decided he needed to be with us all the time, like a real family."

Jenni sat there nodding. She was sweating even though the restaurant was cool from the air conditioning. A part of her rebelled, she didn't want to believe this. "Do you have any proof?"

"Isn't the child enough proof?" Jasmine asked, but she walked back into the kitchen. She returned with a letter in her hand. She passed it over to Jenni. Jenni looked at the envelope. It had been mailed from her own town. The postmark showed a date of five months ago. There was no return address. Her hands were shaking as she pulled the letter from its envelope.

The letter was short and simple, obviously done on a computer.

Dear Jasmine,

It will not be too much longer before we can be together. I hope the house is adequate for the two of you. I will not contact you again until I have final arrangements made.

Love,
Michael

Chapter Thirteen

Jenni folded the letter back up and replaced it in the envelope. She placed it back in Jasmine's waiting hands. "Where is the money he sent you?"

"I don't know anything about any money."

Jenni knew there were things she should ask, but suddenly none of it mattered. Michael had betrayed her. The details didn't matter. Everyone else had been right and she'd been wrong. She'd been so arrogant, so sure that Michael couldn't have done those things, but she'd been wrong.

She stood up and left the restaurant without another word. She walked into the sweltering heat, but her body was chilled. She stood on the sidewalk, not moving, feeling her life crumbling down around her for the second time.

"Jenni."

She turned to the voice. It was Billy Bob. She smiled in surprise, but it turned into fear as the realization dawned that he had called her Jenni, not Caroline.

"What did she tell you?"

Without thinking, Jenni took both her hands and pushed him in the chest hard with all her strength. He fell to the sidewalk. Jenni began to run.

Jasmine sat in the chair, not moving, still clutching her son. He protested at the tightness by pushing away, but she continued to cling to him. She turned and glared at the man that now stood in the doorway that led to the kitchen. The scar under his eye twitched as he watched her. "I did what you wanted. Now, leave us alone."

"You did well, and to show you our gratitude, you get to keep the house and the business, but remember, if she contacts you again, you will tell her the exact same things. And I promise you, we will know if you don't. We don't want to hurt your son, but we do what we have to do."

"You didn't tell me he was dead." Jasmine wiped away the tears.

The man shrugged.

"What kind of monster are you?"

"I'm not a monster at all, just a businessman. And a businessman you might like if you got to know me a little better." He leered at her. She felt sickened by what she'd done, but she had no choice. Her son's safety was more important than any lies she had told. As he walked past her, he brushed against her suggestively. She took several steps away, repulsed by his touch. She stared after him, still clutching her son. She was horrified at the things she'd told that poor woman, but she had to keep her son safe.

Chapter Fourteen

Jenni ran as if her life depended on it, and she thought that it might. She ran down the street and into a side alley. Billy Bob was yelling at her to stop but that only made her run faster. She crossed against the traffic. She heard brakes screeching but did not stop.

Once across the street, she headed into an alley. She looked behind her; he was just coming out of the first alley. He stopped. The flow of traffic was heavy and he had to wait. She turned and ran; she had no time to lose. At the end of that alley, she looked behind her and saw no one. She ran to the right and continued until she saw a clothing store. She ducked into the store.

Her breath was ragged.

"Can I help you, ma'am?" The store clerk was looking at the woman that was breathing so heavily she wondered if she were having a heart attack. "Are you OK?"

Shattered

"Fine," she managed to say between gasps. "Asthma attack—need water."

"Certainly." The store clerk led Jenni to a back room, sat her on a chair with a glass of water, and turned the fan toward her watching her with worry. "Should I call for the hospital?"

Jenni shook her head and managed to gasp out, "No. Just need a minute."

"You just sit here for awhile. I will be out front if you need me."

The man ran out of the alley looking left and right but did not see Jenni. He saw an old woman sitting on the stoop of a storefront. "Did you see a woman run past here?"

She smiled at him. Her smile was toothless. Her skin was dark and wrinkled but her eyes were clear. "No."

"Are you sure?" he demanded.

"I'm old but I'm not blind."

Frustrated, he walked past several of the stores looking for Jenni. He saw nothing. The clerk in the clothing store gave him an inviting wave to come on in.

She waved at the man window shopping hoping he would come in and buy something for a wife, a girlfriend, a mistress, or perhaps something for all three. She chuckled to herself. It wouldn't be the first time. Men could be such pigs.

He smiled at her but went back to the old woman by the alley. Again she assured him she'd seen no one, so he turned back the way he'd come.

Chapter Fourteen

The old woman chuckled to herself after he'd walked away. She knew that a man chasing a woman wasn't a good thing. She would never help a man chasing a woman, not for any reason. She watched the man walking slowly up the alley, checking each locked door as he went. He found an unlocked door, and he stepped into the building.

The clerk walked back to check on the sick woman.

"How are you feeling, ma'am?" A bit of color seemed to have returned to the woman's face, and she was not sweating so profusely as before.

"Much better. Thank you."

"Good, good. This heat can be bad for you if you're not used to it."

"Thank you so much for helping me. I'm feeling stronger now."

They walked around the corner, back to the storefront. Jenni held back, watching to be sure that she didn't see Billy Bob in front of the store. She looked at the clothes that surrounded her. She smiled at the woman watching her.

"I'm here, I might as well do a little shopping, don't you think?"

"We have beautiful clothes."

"I see that." Jenni tried to sound cheerful. She gave a worried look at the window. "The only thing is my husband might be looking for me. We had a fight. That's why I was running and probably why I got sick. I don't want to see him right now. Let him feel bad for awhile."

Shattered

"I did see a man a few minutes ago looking in the window."

"Did he have a ponytail?"

"Yes, I believe he did, but don't worry, he turned around and left."

"Maybe, you can sort of watch out for him while I do a little shopping. If you see him, I just can dash in the back again. In the mood he's in, he certainly wouldn't let me buy anything."

"Sure, sure. Not a problem." The woman walked to the door and stood sentry as Jenni picked out an outfit. Most of the clothes were too flowery for Jenni's tastes, but she finally did find a simple sundress. She added a pair of white sandals and a white straw hat to the ensemble. She looked in the mirror and hoped it would be enough to fool anyone who might be looking for her. She found a big beach bag that she stuffed her old clothes and her trusty tennis shoes in. When the woman gave her the total, Jenni added a hundred-dollar bill.

"I don't want my husband to know I was here."

The woman smiled at the money. "Not a problem, dear. Not a problem at all."

Jenni went to the door and peeked out before opening the door. The last thing she wanted was to walk out into the arms of Billy Bob. She saw no one, so she turned back and thanked the woman one more time and walked out the door. She looked around wondering which way

Chapter Fourteen

to go. She saw an old woman sitting on the stoop of the building. The old woman gave her a toothless smile.

"I don't know who that man was, but I told him you hadn't been this way. He went back down there." She pointed to the alley. "You better go the other way, dear."

Jenni was taken aback by the woman. "Thanks."

"We women have to stick together. Nothing good ever happens when a man is chasing a woman, you know."

"You're right about that. Thanks." Jenni turned and walked past the store. She didn't know where to go, but she couldn't go back to the hotel.

She kept walking until she found herself back at the ocean. It looked like a commercial area, lots of boats, and she watched as she saw fish being hauled off of boats and others coming up to the fisherman haggling over prices but finally buying the fisherman's product.

She sat on the grass watching the scene in front of her. She needed to get off this island. All she had with her was her purse and her passport, but that was all she needed. She walked to the pier. At the first boat, she stopped and said, "Hi."

The man looked up but had an expression of annoyance at the interruption.

"Hello."

"I need to get to another island. Can you help me?"

"And why would you need to do that?"

"I had a fight with my husband." It had worked with the store clerk, so she might as well stick to that story.

Shattered

"Go to the airport."

"He'll find me there. I can pay."

The man stood up and stretched his back as he thought about it. "I can't do it, but I heard George talking about going to Bimminy later today. You can ask him." He pointed further down the pier. "It's the one called *Paradise*."

Jenni thanked the man profusely, but he'd already turned back to his work. She walked down the pier until she came to a boat that had *Paradise* written on the side. She looked at the boat doubtfully. Certainly the man hadn't meant this boat.

Paradise was anything but paradise. All the paint had worn off long ago showing only the weathered wood of the beat-up boat. The name had apparently been repainted on the boat by hand. The letters were crooked. The boat didn't look like it would even run, let alone be safe for the ocean. Just then a man came up from the hold.

He looked at her looking at his boat. He had a defiant look about him, as if he just wanted her to say something bad about his boat.

"Are you George?"

"Who wants to know?"

"The man up there told me you were going to Bimini today and that you might let me go with you."

"And why would you need to go to Bimini with George?"

Chapter Fourteen

"I'm mad at my husband, and I want to teach him a lesson."

The man looked at her for several seconds with an intense scowl and then began to laugh, a loud belly laugh. "Then, I am George."

George was as black as ebony. His skin was so black that it appeared to shine much like ebony. His teeth were as white as his skin was black. George was a big man, certainly close to six-foot-five. His frame was large but strongly built. He was bald. He looked like what Jenni imagined a pirate might look like.

Jenni gave him a tentative smile back.

"I will pay you."

"Fine, fine, but I must warn you we will be fishing along the way."

"That's OK."

"You don't look dressed to fish, but OK. You are lucky. I was just about to leave. Come aboard."

He walked to where Jenni was standing. She put out a hand to have him help her aboard, but instead he placed his hands under her armpits and swung her onto the boat in one graceful movement. Being aboard the ship did nothing to reassure Jenni that *Paradise* was ocean worthy, but she was going to Bimini as long as the ship didn't sink along the way.

George yelled over his shoulder at her, "You might want to sit in there, out of the sun." He pointed to where the ship's steering wheel was. As she sat down on the bench, which was just a wooden box, she could feel the seat giving at her weight. She wondered how the old crate could tolerate George's weight. The smell of fish was noticeable, but surely once they were moving the ocean breeze would take care of the offensive odor.

George was wandering around the boat doing things she didn't understand. He hummed as he moved about the boat. After a few minutes, the odor of the fish began to overpower her. She felt her stomach tightening into a fist. Jenni decided to go back on deck hoping that fresh air would help.

She walked out from under the makeshift shelter into the sweltering heat—not even a hint of a breeze—but she could still smell the fish even if she couldn't see them. People could see her from the pier. She went back to the crate.

A smiling George jumped on the boat, and Jenni swore she felt the boards giving way under his considerable weight. She gave him back a shaky smile.

"Time to go." He turned on the engine, and Jenni held her breath, positive the old thing wouldn't start but it did, and to her amazement on the first try. She watched as George maneuvered the fishing boat out of its place. He seemed to know what he was doing, not that Jenni would know if he didn't. She knew nothing about boats, especially working fishing boats.

Once they got moving, the breeze did help with the fishy smell, but it didn't take it completely away. After

Chapter Fourteen

about twenty-five minutes, George stopped the boat and put out a large net, a net bigger than anything Jenni had ever seen. When he finished, he turned toward Jenni, the first sign that he remembered she was on the boat.

"So, you are mad at your husband, huh? What did he do?"

Jenni wasn't much for lying, but as long as she had to she figured she might as well go all the way. "We came down here for a vacation. We've been having trouble." She rolled her eyes. "Marital troubles. He said that it would be a second honeymoon—that we would work things out. Then, I find he brought his girlfriend down, too. That was it, no more."

George chuckled. "These American men, they have the nerve. If I did something like that, my wife would make sure that I never . . . well let's just say it wouldn't be pleasant, if you know what I mean. So, what will you do now?"

"Spend a few day here and then go home and find the best divorce lawyer I can find. He can have his mistress, but let's just see if she wants him when he's poor."

George chuckled again, and Jenni felt pleased with herself; not only had she sounded believable but George had enjoyed the story. She asked him about his family, and he explained that he only saw his family on Sundays. The rest of the time he was working, but Sundays were always a good day. His wife was a good woman and a good cook. His children were good children, but

Shattered

the oldest boy did get in to trouble occasionally. Next year he would begin to learn the business with George.

After about thirty minutes of slowly moving across the ocean, they stopped and George began to turn a handle. Jenni saw that it was moving the net up. George turned to her. "A lot of the fishermen now use electrical equipment to pull in the fish, but I like doing it myself. I don't want to be a machine operator, I want to be a fisherman."

With that pronouncement, he began to pull in the net. Jenni could see his muscles straining as he worked to pull the fish and heavy net into the boat. Then the fish were in the boat with her. She lifted her feet as they scattered about the deck. Her stomach began to tighten. She closed her eyes trying not to breathe.

She became aware of the boat rocking, back and forth, back and forth. She opened her eyes. The world looked tilted. She tried to ignore the queasiness. She took deep breaths, willing her stomach to behave. The deep breaths only succeeded in making her more aware of the fish. She rushed to the side of the boat losing the battle with her stomach.

She was mortified, but there was nothing she could do but lean further over the side and heave. She felt her hat fly off. The heaving didn't seem to bring any relief. She could feel the swaying of the boat bringing on a bout of dizziness. More heaving. The hot, foul-smelling air pressed against her. More heaving. She felt a comforting hand on her back.

Chapter Fourteen

"Close your eyes. Don't open them and keep breathing."

She did as she was told. The hand kept rubbing her back. After a few minutes, the heaving stopped. She continued to make herself breathe, as if her body had forgotten how to.

"Don't open those eyes."

His large hands guided her, she walked with eyes closed, and then he gently helped her to lie down. She kept breathing and kept her eyes closed. She drifted off to sleep. She opened her eyes, momentarily confused. Then, she smelled the fish and remembered. She looked around for George.

She found him standing at the stern guiding the boat.

"I see you're awake, and it's a good thing; we will be coming in to port in just a few minutes."

"I am so sorry. I've never gotten sick on a boat before."

"Have you ever been on a fishing boat before?"

"No, but . . ."

"Well, there you go. It's not your fault"

"I lied to you. I'm sorry." The words were out before she even realized that she was going to say them. "You're a very nice man. I shouldn't have lied."

George nodded but didn't speak.

She went on talking telling him all that had happened to her. She left nothing out, not even the newly found son. Somewhere in the middle of her speech, his eyes softened as he listened to her story. When she was finished, she stood staring at him.

Shattered

"It's OK." He patted her shoulder. "You have had a rough time of it. It sounds to me as if you still have many troubles to take care of. I don't like lying, but you certainly did need to get off that island. What will you do now?"

Jenni shook her head. "I don't know. Do you have any ideas?"

"Mmm. This sounds very dangerous. Your husband may not have been completely innocent in this matter, but there are others chasing you now. That is not your husband's doing. Maybe you should call the police"

"They think I'm crazy." She shrugged. "Who knows? Maybe I am the crazy one."

"I don't think so," George answered slowly. He said nothing for a long time, and then he turned to her. "It seems you have two choices. One, you can keep trying to find the truth and probably get killed in the process, or two, you must make them accept that you now believe the story. If these people think you will stop looking into the matter, then they might just decide to leave you alone. You will not be a threat to them any longer."

She started to protest but he held up a hand.

"I know there is more to this story, but your safety must come first."

She twisted at the ring knowing that "gmfl" was etched inside. Michael had broken the promise. She owed him nothing any longer.

Chapter Fourteen

After they'd landed, George walked her to a small restaurant by the pier. It was a place for locals by the looks of it. She saw the questioning looks in their eyes as she walked in still aided by George. Hers was the only white face in the restaurant. George helped her to a table and then went up and whispered a few words to the waitress.

Jenni saw the waitress smiling and bobbing her head as she glanced at Jenni, still listening to George. George came to the table and sat down. "She's going to bring you food that will help your stomach. I have to get back to my fish before they spoil."

Jenni stood up. "Thanks so much for helping me. And I'm sorry I got sick in your boat."

"Not a problem."

"How much for the trip?"

George shook his head. "Nothing at all. That would hardly be fair; you got sick. You didn't even get to enjoy the ocean."

"All the more reason to let me pay you. No one should have to deal with a sick woman while they're trying to fish."

"No, no."

"I insist."

"Fine, ten dollars would be fair."

Jenni reached in her purse and handed him a folded hundred-dollar bill. She put it in his hand and stretched to give him a hug. "Thanks so much for everything."

Shattered

He smiled. "Not a problem. If you need to escape again, look me up." He walked away, chuckling. Jenni sat back down, alone again. The waitress brought a bowl with crackers.

"It's just chicken broth. Use a lot of crackers. It will help."

Jenni nodded and began to crumble crackers into the broth. Once Jenni began to eat, she realized she was hungry and finished the bowl. Her stomach felt more settled, and she could feel strength returning to her limbs. Chicken broth did cure what ailed a body.

While paying at the register Jenni asked the woman about a taxi. The woman went to the phone and called a taxi. Jenni stepped outside to wait for the taxi and was immediately assaulted by the heat. She took a deep breath; she could still smell the fish but from a distance.

The taxi driver took her to a small hotel out of town that was by the beach. He talked the whole drive, but Jenni couldn't focus on what he was saying, so she just made attentive sounds.

She registered, and this time she remembered not to sign in under her own name. She walked to her air-conditioned room and lay on the bed. She expected to lie awake in bed but instead fell into a deep sleep.

The next morning as she opened her eyes scenes of the past morning flashed before her. Jasmine DuPree holding the letter, Michael's son running into the room,

Chapter Fourteen

Billy Bob calling her by her name and chasing her. Her mind went back to the child, Michael's child.

She'd been pregnant once, and they were so excited at the prospects of having a family. They had been so full of hope then. She'd grown up as an only child, often lonely having no one to laugh and giggle with, no one to share secrets with. She and Michael had wanted a big family.

Michael had pampered her and barely let her walk to the bathroom without assistance. He'd hired someone to clean house leaving her with nothing to do during the day but read, sleep, and eat, which was a good thing since she seem to be sick so much of the time.

She'd sat in the rocking chair in the evenings and watched him fix up the nursery. He never seemed too tired to work on it even though he'd worked all day. She watched him peel off layers of old wallpaper and put up the Mickey Mouse paper they'd both agreed would be theme of the room. They'd chosen Mickey Mouse since it was gender neutral. He hung mobiles from the ceiling. He sanded the wood floor and then changed his mind and had it carpeted anyway. When he was finished, the room was adorable.

Jenni tightened her arms around herself in a hug; she could still feel the ache of wanting to hold her baby even after all these years. It had been in her seventh month and she'd called the doctor to complain that she didn't feel right, she was achy and had cramps. He'd

Shattered

assured her that it was normal but told her to come in and see him anyway, but before she got there the bleeding began. She drove herself to the emergency room.

When she'd awakened in the hospital, she knew by the looks on everyone's faces that she'd lost their baby. At the time, she'd thought she'd never smile or laugh again, but time had healed the wound. Her second and third pregnancies had been joyous but restrained. It was if they were holding their breath during those pregnancies, as if that could make the difference, but it hadn't and both of those pregnancies ended the same way the first one had.

The doctor explained that it would be difficult for her to carry a baby to term but not impossible with a lot of luck. Michael had held her then and cried for both of them. She was beyond tears. He'd told her he loved her and absolutely refused to put her through another pregnancy. She'd tried to make him change his mind, but he wouldn't, and he'd proved it to her over and over, and now they were saying it was all lies.

Michael had worked hard to bring the joy back into their lives after the decision not to have children had been made. He'd insisted that she was all he needed to make his life complete, and so there had been no more pregnancies. He'd cajoled her into getting more involved in their community, and it had helped. She'd volunteered at hospitals, schools, and other organizations that needed her.

Chapter Fourteen

And in the end he had planned to leave her for his child. She wanted to hate him for that but she didn't. She didn't even blame him for that. It wasn't wrong for him to want to take care of his son. The thought started the tears, and for the next twenty-four hours she lay in bed taking turns crying and sleeping.

Crying because Michael had betrayed her, she'd told everyone he wouldn't have done that, but he had. Crying because she didn't know whom she could trust. Crying because she didn't know how to fix the mess she was in.

By the next afternoon she was done crying and done feeling sorry for herself. For the next several days, she took walks on the beach and chatted about inconsequential matters with other tourists. She'd put away her problems for the moment, but her mind silently worked on the riddle. *How do I get out of this mess?*

She lay on a chaise lounge listening to the waves and happy children sounds. It surprised her that she could look at the children without feeling sorry for herself. God was slowly healing her heart and her mind.

It was time to take charge of her life. She was tired of being manipulated. She was taking back her life, such as it was. She was ready to move forward. It still hurt and probably always would, but she was alive and she wouldn't waste the life that God had given her.

A son would be the only reason in the world that Michael would have violated his principles. She just didn't understand why Michael needed to steal money

Shattered

in the process. They had more than enough money for both of them to live separately, but she knew there would always be unanswered questions.

She would have let him go. She wouldn't have stopped him even if it had broken her heart. But one can never understand fully another person's reasoning, so she wasn't going to drive herself crazy asking questions that she would never know the answers to.

The biggest question was why Michael had killed himself when he was arrested. His son still needed him. Michael's faith wouldn't have allowed him to kill himself. She just couldn't believe that of him. It didn't make sense.

Her mind froze.

A light bulb came on. It didn't make sense because he hadn't killed himself. She was sure that she'd been right all along about that. If Michael had stolen the money and killed himself, then why was she on this island hiding from someone? Why had Billy Bob chased her? How had he known her name?

Michael had not been acting alone. That was clear. Someone else had been involved. If Michael had lived, he would have been able to tell the whole story. His accomplice would have been arrested. Billy Bob might be the accomplice, or Billy Bob might be working for Michael's accomplice. His accomplice had somehow succeeded in drugging Michael and inducing the heart attack.

That same accomplice now felt that she posed a danger to him. It was only after she began to search for the

Chapter Fourteen

truth that someone had been pulling strings from behind the scenes trying to stop her.

She had two choices just as George had told her days ago, she could continue to work to expose the accomplice, or she could give up and be safe. Did she still owe it to Michael to expose his murderer? She'd told George that she didn't owe Michael anything, but she wasn't sure that was the truth.

All of her being screamed that she wanted to find the person who killed Michael, but it wasn't just her safety she had to be concerned with. She had to think of Michael's son, she didn't want him to be hurt.

She made her decision.

She stood up and walked into the ocean to cool off. The warmth of the tropical water loosened her muscles. She relaxed. The water was an astonishing shade of turquoise blue that blended into the horizon separated only by the white caps of the waves. She tasted the salt that was burning her eyes. She heard children's giggles over the waves. She smiled.

Jenni went back to her beach chair. She thought about what she needed to do. She had to get a message to whomever wanted to stop her from learning the truth. She had to find a way to let them know that she wasn't a threat any longer. She didn't know who the accomplice was, but she did know some of the people who had been involved with her since Michael's death: Nicholas Peyton, Annie Meyers, Carmen and Roberto, her mother, and of course Dr. Rinaldi.

That was it. She would call Dr. Rinaldi. She wasn't just an innocent doctor trying to help Jenni. Jenni had no doubt that Dr. Rinaldi had been drugging her while she was at the clinic. Dr. Rinaldi was definitely involved in some way. She would also call her mother.

She knew her mother wasn't involved, but she had allowed herself to be used by someone. That person was certainly still in touch with her mother hoping to find out where Jenni was. If Jenni could convince both Dr. Rinaldi and her mother that she believed what the police were saying, then she might be safe. If she were safe, then Michael's son would be safe.

She went to her room to make phone calls.

Chapter Fifteen

Jenni walked off the plane slowly. She had no idea if her two phone calls had worked their magic. She prayed that they had; otherwise, she didn't know what she would do. She was tired of all the turmoil and drama. All she wanted was to go home and grieve.

She felt more at peace than she would have thought possible. She was coming to terms with Michael's betrayal. She finally understood that with God's help, all things truly are possible, even the healing of a broken heart. It hurt, but she could understand Michael wanting to be with his son. As for his suicide, she didn't believe that for a moment, but she was at peace with her decision to stop her search for the truth.

She hadn't told her mother exactly when she would be arriving. When she called her mother, she told her about Michael's son and how it all made sense. It took some doing, but she did finally did succeed in calming

Shattered

her mother down. Jenni did the same when she talked with Gail Rinaldi.

She wanted a few days to herself to adjust to the task of living without Michael. Once safely in her house, Jenni sighed with relief. She walked around the house touching things, they looked the same, and yet everything was different. She sighed again. Nothing would ever be the same again.

Jenni pushed the sad thoughts away. She was determined not to wallow in self-pity, and with God's help she would rebuild her life. She didn't know exactly what she wanted to do with that life, but whatever it was, it would be done for God's glory.

Jenni walked around her house finding small chores to keep her occupied. If she kept busy, then she didn't have to think. She walked to the refrigerator and found that there was no usable food in the house. She cleaned out the spoiled food and then went grocery shopping.

It felt odd to do such mundane chores. After putting the groceries away and eating a ham and cheese sandwich, she looked at the pile of mail that had been collecting since she went into Gail Rinaldi's clinic.

Her mother hadn't done anything with it other than to pile it up. She looked at the pile with distaste. It would mostly be outdated bills and perhaps a few condolence cards. She didn't want to deal with any of it. Without looking at any of it, she threw it in the trash. Anything important would be sent to her again, and she would

Chapter Fifteen

call up the utilities and explain the situation and ask for new bills to be sent.

She picked up a book and went to the porch to sit and read. She tried to focus on the words but wasn't successful. She heard a noise and looked up. It was Mr. Gamble.

Mr. Gamble had been their mailman since they'd lived in this house. Jenni didn't understand why he hadn't retired yet. It was obvious; he was far past retirement age. He moved slowly and their mail was always late. He gave her a warm wave as he made his way up her walk.

"Mrs. Hamilton, you're back. I've missed you so."

"Morning, Mr. Gamble."

He gave her a friendly pat on her shoulder. "How are you doing? I know it can be pretty rough when you lose your husband or wife."

"I'm OK." She felt tears spring to her eyes.

"You know I lost my Patty several years ago. Didn't think I could make it but I did, and I've got me a lady friend now." He shook his head and gave her a wry smile. "Who would have thought it?"

"I'm just trying to get through each day."

"That's a good way to start. Well, I know you've got plenty of mail to keep you busy for a few days now that you're back." He handed her a small stack of mail. "Here's some more to add to that pile."

Shattered

She shook her head. "Not really. When I saw that pile, I just threw it all out and decided I'd start with whatever you brought today."

He frowned.

"Is something wrong, Mr. Gamble?"

"Well, I can understand your sentiment, but I couldn't help but notice a letter that had been mailed from some other country." He stopped talking. "Mmm. Can't seem to remember what country, but it looked important."

Her eyes widened. "Are you sure? I don't know anyone that would send me something from overseas."

He scratched his head and looked off in to space as if trying to conjure up the image. "Seems to me it was from one of those islands down in the Caribbean, but I can't remember which one."

Jenni smiled hoping she didn't look as anxious as she felt. "That will teach me to throw everything away without looking for it. I guess I'm going to be digging through my garbage. Thanks, Mr. Gamble."

Jenni hurried into the house. There was only one island and only one person on that island that had any reason to write her. She rushed to the kitchen to the trash, only to remember that she had taken the garbage out to the garage to await pick-up day.

She stood looking at the coffee grounds that she had dumped on top of the mail. Well, it couldn't be helped. She started rooting through the mail trying not

Chapter Fifteen

to notice the rotting smell of the food that had spoiled while she'd been gone. Luckily, that was at the bottom of the bag. After a few more minutes, she found the mail that she'd ditched.

She dragged all the mail back in with her. She decided she'd better go through all of it. She sat down at the kitchen table with a cup of coffee. She rifled through the envelopes until she found the one she was looking for. There was no return address on it, but the postage stamps said the Bahamas.

Why had Jasmine DuPree written her? Jasmine had already broken her heart once; that should be enough for her. Why was she tormenting Jenni? Jenni debated about whether she really wanted to read what that woman had to say, but she knew she wouldn't be able to resist.

She had no choice. She had to know what the woman wanted from her now. Jenni ripped open the envelope and began reading.

> Please forgive me. I have committed a sin against you and against my son's father. The things I told you were lies. I had no choice; my son was in danger. But I could not live with myself. I only saw Michael that one night and even then he told me that he loved you. I never saw him again. Several months ago I wrote him a letter asking for help and I soon received money to buy the restaurant. Soon after that I got a deed to my house. I received letters

but none of them were signed by his hand. They were only typed. I never spoke to Michael. At the time, I believed they were from him, but now I do not believe so. I believe those evil people used me and my son, but I do not know why. I beg you not to tell anyone of this letter, as they told me they would come back and kill my son if I ever contacted you. My brother-in-law mailed this for me so as not to endanger my son. I am so sorry. Please forgive me.

The letter fell from Jenni's hands as she slid to the floor. She sat staring at the letter. She picked it up and reread it several times. She sobbed. Michael had not betrayed her. He wasn't going to leave her. He had kept his promise. He hadn't been going to leave her. He had loved her and only her.

She felt an anger ignite inside her and with every thought, every breath, the anger grew. They would pay for murdering Michael. She stood up and read the letter one more time. She went and found matches in her junk drawer and went to the sink. She lit the edge of the letter and then the envelope and watched them burn.

She turned on the faucet and watched the water swirl away any evidence of the letter. *Michael, Michael, what should I do? How can I prove your innocence?* She tapped her foot. She knew what Michael's answer would be: "Don't do it. Forget about it."

He would want her to be safe, but she didn't want to be safe. There must be something that could prove

Chapter Fifteen

Michael's innocence. Where would Michael have hidden important papers?

She already knew they weren't in the safety deposit box at the bank. Roberto had helped her with those papers while planning the funeral. She would go over every inch of the house. There had to be something in the house that could help her prove Michael was innocent.

She called a moving company and arranged to have boxes delivered. She sat at the kitchen table drinking coffee trying to calm down. Trying to form a plan, but she could think no further ahead than searching the house for some clue.

Once the boxes arrived, she began in their bedroom. She folded and put his clothes in the boxes; she meticulously went through each pocket. She stopped from time to time as she came across an item that would bring on a wave of new memories. They were good memories now that she knew Michael hadn't betrayed her.

For the first time since Michael's death, she could trust completely in him and in their love. She didn't have to hide from their love any longer. It had been real. No, she corrected herself. It *was* real.

Several hours later she stopped when she heard the doorbell ring. The bedroom had been stripped bare of all Michael's things. Her shoulders and back hurt, and she still hadn't found anything to help her. She had even gone so far as to check the back of each picture frame and bottoms of the drawers, nothing.

Shattered

The doorbell rang again. She worried about how she must look. Between the dust and the crying, her eyes felt red and raw. She peeked out the window and saw her mother standing there. *Alone, thank God.* Jenni wanted to scream at her to go away but knew better.

She didn't want to end up back at the hospital with Dr. Rinaldi. She needed people to believe that she had accepted their lies as truth. She walked downstairs and opened the door. Her mother grabbed her and began crying. Jenni was the one comforting her when it should have been the other way around, but it had always been that way with them.

When her mother finally stopped crying, she gave Jenni a look.

"Are you OK? You look awful."

"I'm OK. It's been a bad afternoon. I'm going through Michael's things and packing them up to give away. It was harder than I thought it would be, but it needed to be done. I wanted his things out of here as soon as possible."

"Let me help you."

"No." The word came out more sharply than Jenni intended. She gave her mother a smile. "This is something I need to do. I have to put the past behind me, and no one can help me do that. I have to do it by myself."

"It's hard, baby. But you'll feel better when you're done."

"Let me take a quick shower, then I'll cook dinner."

Chapter Fifteen

"Better yet. You go take the shower and I'll cook. Anything in particular?"

"I have hamburger in the refrigerator for spaghetti and meatballs and the makings of a salad."

After her shower, they ate together. And surprisingly, there were no arguments. She told her mother about Michael's son again and about the incident when she thought the man was following her and how that had led to the realization that she'd had some sort of breakdown. She went on to tell her about the boat ride and how she'd spent those days in the hotel sleeping and getting herself together.

Chapter Sixteen

After her mother left, Jenni went to Michael's den. She looked around, overwhelmed at the thought that Michael would never sit at his desk again. His presence in the room was palpable. She felt as if she could hear him breathing just behind her, but she knew it was just an illusion.

It felt like an invasion of his privacy to search through his things in this room. They'd always been very conscientious of respecting each other's privacy. She went over to Michael's sound system; he'd always get aggravated when she called the humongous monstrosity a stereo. She hit *Play* on the CD player. This was the last music that Michael had ever listened to as he sat in this room.

She smiled as she listened. It didn't surprise her that it was Springsteen. Vintage Springsteen, Michael would say, the good stuff. But all his music is good, he would

Shattered

explain. It's just that his early music is classic rock-and-roll at its best.

Jenni sat down on the carpet and lost herself in memories. They'd gone to all his concerts that had come to town. They traveled from city to city following Bruce and attending his concerts. It was their own version of being a Dead Head. They'd slept in sleeping bags when the weather was nice and in the car when it wasn't. He'd asked her to marry him the day of the last concert of that summer. It had been a great summer.

She stretched out on the carpet and closed her eyes. She felt Michael's arms around her, the warmth of his body against her. She knew he would stay with her as long as she kept her eyes closed. He whispered in her ear, "Don't do this. It's too dangerous. Forget about it."

She almost opened her eyes but didn't want him to leave. She whispered back to him, "I have to do this. I won't let them get away with killing you."

"It doesn't matter. I'm gone and I want you to stay safe. God has plans for you." She felt his warm breath on her neck.

"It does matter," she cried. "It matters to me. I want you back with me. I don't know how to live without you."

"I will always be with you, Jenni, my love. Be happy."

"Don't go." She reached out but felt the warmth of his body slip away. She opened her eyes and looked around the empty room. She'd fallen asleep.

Chapter Sixteen

She looked around the room, ready to work again. Bruce's voice sang on. She began with the desk drawers. She read each piece of paper and threw out some papers, but kept the important ones but found nothing that could give her a clue she needed.

Jenni pounded her head on the desktop in frustration but refused to give up. She felt under the drawers and then actually sat on the floor to see if there was anything taped to the underside of the desk or the drawers, nothing. She went to the antique TV set that Michael had converted into a safe. She took the laptop computer out of the TV safe and waited for it to boot up. She went back to the TV and peered in to be sure it was empty.

Then, she had a thought. *Michael had been so proud of his hidden safe. Could he have made another hidden compartment and not told me?* She began pushing and pulling on every part of the TV. Nothing happened. She tried lifting the bottom of the entire compartment. It didn't budge. She ran her fingers around the edge hoping to trigger movement. Nothing happened, but she felt something stuck in the crack.

She pulled it out. It was a business card. She looked at it with disappointment. It was a plain card with a name and number only. No company name or company logo on it. The name was William Robert Gindlesburger.

She couldn't remember Michael mentioning the name. She sat there on the floor trying to jog her memory but couldn't come up with anything. It was probably an

Shattered

old business associate of Michael's whose card had just slipped between the cracks, literally. She tossed the card in the trash.

It was late; Jenni didn't want to stop but she was exhausted. She was sure she would find the clue she needed in this room. She went to the computer and began to examine word processing files but found nothing that would help her.

It was after four in the morning. She had to get some sleep. She would check the rest of the files the next day. It wouldn't do any good to continue. She was so tired that she would miss any clues that she did come across.

She felt as if she had a hangover when she woke up the next morning. Lack of sleep. She forced herself to eat before she went back to the office. She booted up the laptop and began to check each file on the hard disk. When she was finished, she knew nothing more than when she started except that Michael was apparently a computer game junkie, and she hadn't known that.

She thought back to the times she'd come in and he would hasten to hit buttons and then reassure her that she wasn't interrupting him at all. At the time, she had believed he hadn't want her to see his work, but now she was wondering if he hadn't wanted her to see that he was playing games.

She went down to eat something. She checked her answering machine as her soup heated in the microwave. There were messages from her mother, Carmen,

Chapter Sixteen

and Dr. Rinaldi. Jenni made a face as she listened to that monotone voice that she had grown to hate while she was stuck in that clinic. She knew she should call them back, but she wasn't in the mood.

Back in the office she searched the closets and found nothing. She sat at Michael's desk, clicking her nails on the wood, not sure how to proceed. She went over to the sound system and began to straighten up the mess that Michael had left. He loved his music but was never a stickler when it came to neatness. There were CDs tossed carelessly in a pile on top of the CD player.

She began to put them in their plastic holders and then put them in empty spaces in the CD rack. She found the Springsteen CD case of the music she'd listened to the night before. The case wasn't empty. Just like Michael to have the wrong CD in the case. She opened it up to check the label so she could put it in the right holder. There was no label on it.

That was odd. She replaced the Springsteen CD with the unlabeled CD and turned it on. Nothing happened. She took it back out and looked at it. She glanced at the laptop and wondered if this could be a CD for a computer.

She felt a tingle. This could be what she'd been looking for. It would be just like Michael to have tossed it carelessly into his pile of CDs. He always said the best place to hide something was in plain sight. Apparently,

Shattered

the police hadn't bothered looking through the pile of music CDs.

She slipped the CD into the drive. She heard it whirring as it loaded into the computer. She waited barely able to breathe. A message flashed on the screen, it said, "no carrier." At first, the message puzzled her, and then she realized that the modem needed to be attached to a phone line. She took the phone jack and stuck it in the back of the computer and then double-clicked again and waited.

She heard the connection, but then a message flashed asking for a password. The password for their Internet server was Michael's middle name and his birth year, Albert 1955. She shrugged and typed it hoping it would be the same, but the message flashed back at her, "access denied." She sat there clicking her fingernails on the desk trying to think what he might have used.

She thought about where she'd found the CD. Again back to his theory: make it simple and most people won't get it. She typed in bruce. Nothing happened. She typed in all sorts of combinations that would make sense. Nothing happened. She thought for a minute and added his birth date but nothing happened. Then she added her birth date.

She hit Enter and the next page popped up. It was obvious this was a program for serious users, no flashy graphics. It could have passed for a word-processing program.

Chapter Sixteen

She moved the cursor up to the top toolbar and hit File. It revealed three choices: New Mail, Read Mail, Sent Mail. She moved the cursor to New Mail and double-clicked.

A message flashed asking for another password. This program certainly was security conscious. She thought for a moment and typed in Albert 1955, their old password. She hit Enter. A date appeared on the monitor. The day before Michael had died. Her pulse raced. She double-clicked and waited for the file to open. There was only one sentence: "Will meet you at noon at mall. BB"

She read the cryptic sentence and something niggled in her brain as she looked at the message. She shook her head. *Who was BB and why was Michael meeting him?* An idea popped in her head and without thinking about the consequences, she hit the reply button and typed: "Meet me at the mall at noon tomorrow. Michael's wife."

She hit Send before she could change her mind. She could almost feel the message pulsing through the phone lines. She left the program on in case she got a response to the e-mail. She'd found what she'd been looking for. Now all she could do was wait.

The man was surprised to see an incoming message flashing on that account. Michael Hamilton had been dead for some time. The only reason the account was still active was that he had neglected to cancel it. He read the message and frowned. He didn't like what the message implied. He thought about answering the mes-

Shattered

sage but in the end decided that the safest thing was to do nothing.

In another building across town, a person frowned at the beep that signified activity on Michael Hamilton's e-mail account. The cursor moved down and was double clicked on the flashing window. This wasn't good news. Someone would need to be told and something would have to be done. Why hadn't Jenni left well enough alone? She'd told everyone that she was done with her search for the truth. She'd told everyone that she believed the police. That obviously wasn't the truth.

After Jenni hit the Send button, she needed to keep busy. She didn't want to think about the consequences of what she'd done. She was positive that it would shake some trees, but she didn't want to think about what might happen. If it was a mistake, then it was a mistake, but there was nothing to be done now but to wait.

She went to the garage and found the pruner and went to work on the overgrown bushes that had been badly neglected for most of the summer. It felt good to be doing something constructive. With each snip, she could see her accomplishment fall to the ground.

That evening she made a point to make some long overdue calls to friends and family. She even called Dr. Rinaldi. She assured one and all that she was fine and ready to get on with her life. The last thing she wanted was interference from well-meaning people again.

Chapter Sixteen

She had been checking the e-mail throughout the day, but no response had appeared. She thought about the initials BB and wondered what it was about them that bothered her, but she could think of nothing.

After a tense night of pacing between the computer and watching TV, she decided a long, luxurious bath with lots of bubbles was what she needed. She went to Michael's room and turned on the CD player. She took a glass of wine with her. It would do her good to relax. She lit candles and turned off the lights.

The man had been watching the house all evening. Finally the lights went off. He smiled in the dark; it was about time. He pushed his hair out of the way and opened the door. It was time to go to work. He didn't understand why he couldn't just kill her and be done with it. She was a pain in the neck but the bosses said no. That might throw suspicion on them. If they could just get her to accept Michael's death, then that would be the end of it.

Jenni dipped a toe in the bubbles to test the water temperature, perfect. She tossed off the towel and slid into the tub in one graceful movement. The bubbles went up to her chin. She sighed and reached for the wine. The cold Zinfandel was a perfect complement to the heat of the bath water. The music from the classical CD made wonderful background music as she sank further into the hot water and the bubbles. She took an-

Shattered

other sip of wine, closed her eyes, and let Beethoven soothe her soul.

The man stood in front of the house that was directly behind Jenni Hamilton's house. The problem was he could hear the barking of a dog in the backyard and he hadn't even started up the drive yet. He kept walking past the house; he could not let the police be alerted. He turned and walked back to his car. It would have to be Plan B.

He went back to the car and moved it. He gave the neighborhood time to tuck themselves in and then once again he began walking, but this time he walked directly to Jenni's house. He walked down the darkened street as if he belonged. As he approached Jenni's house, he scanned her neighbors' houses and saw nothing. Without any hesitation, he hurried up the drive and to the backyard.

The neighbor's dog began barking furiously. He cursed himself for not having the foresight to bring meat to quiet the dog. He should have known this neighborhood would be full of noisy dogs that had nothing better to do than create commotion just when he didn't want them to.

Jenni heard the neighbor dog barking. That dog spent most of his time barking at everything, including his own shadow, but it was a marshmallow. The dog wouldn't hurt a flea.

Chapter Sixteen

Her water had grown tepid. She finished the last sip of wine and stepped out of the tub. She wrapped herself in a giant maroon towel and began to blow dry her hair, which only took a few minutes thanks to her new style.

The dog was still barking ferociously, and it sounded to Jenni as if the dog was seriously upset. She shut off the bathroom light and went from window to window checking for anything unusual. Just as she thought, the dog was being its usual nervous self.

She went to her bedroom and slipped on a nightgown. She walked to the office to check for new e-mail; she promised herself it would be the last time that night. She'd driven herself crazy checking it since she had sent the message to BB earlier that day.

She sighed. *Nothing new.*

She stood remembering the feeling when she'd listened to Springsteen. She knew it was crazy, but she'd felt Michael there with her. She took out the CD and slipped in one of The Boss's. The house didn't feel so lonely. She sat in front of the sound system and hoped she could recapture that feeling.

He stood in the shadows that the darkness provided waiting for the dog to shut up. He cursed his own stupidity for not having thought of bringing something to calm the dog down. He should have known there'd be lots of dogs in a family neighborhood like this. Eventually, his patience was rewarded. The neighborhood quieted again. He moved silently and confidently through

Shattered

the darkness to the door. He knew the house. He'd been here before.

He took the key chain from his pocket, slid the first key into the lock, and heard it click open. He smiled and moved down to the second lock. He was thankful that Jenni had never taken the time to get a security system or to change the locks since Michael's death.

He turned the knob and opened the door. He smiled. He heard the blare of rock-and-roll music from above and smiled. The music would mask the sounds of his footsteps. He navigated through the darkened house taking care not to bump into anything. The last thing he needed was to alert Jenni to his presence until he was ready to do so.

At the bottom of the stairs, he stood and listened. He discerned no movement nor any light, just the music. He wondered if she was in bed and the music was to help her sleep. He moved silently up the stairs.

Jenni opened her eyes and looked around the room. She shivered. She listened but heard nothing over the sound of the music, not even the dog barking. Something felt wrong. Her hand went to shut off the music, but then she thought better of it.

She stood up and moved silently to the office door. She listened but heard nothing. She opened the door and waited. Still nothing. She stepped out into the hall and detected a form moving down the hall. The shadow saw her at the same time.

Chapter Sixteen

Jenni ran back into the office and slammed the door shut with the intention of locking it, but his strength overpowered her. She let go of the door and raced for the phone. It was in her hand, but he wrenched it from her before she could dial. She pivoted and pressed with all her strength. She managed to push him away from her. She ran for the door.

His body came flying toward her as if they were engaged in a bizarre football game and he was tackling her. She landed on the floor and he on top of her. She screamed hoping to alert a neighbor, but his hand over her mouth stifled the scream before it had even started.

She bit at his hand but wasn't successful. She lay on the floor gasping for air praying for the strength to push him off of her.

"I'm not going to hurt you, Jenni. Just relax." The man kept repeating the phrase like a mantra until Jenni finally listened to him. She focused in on the voice and then the face. She stared in shock and things began to fall in place.

He must have felt her relax because he loosened his iron grip on her mouth just a bit. She took a breath to scream, but his hand tightened over her mouth again.

"Jenni, look at me. I am not going to hurt you. Just don't yell. I can't afford to have the police come investigating." He gave her an intense look. "I'm going to move my hand, but you have to nod that you won't scream. I promise I'm not here to hurt you. I just want to talk to you."

Shattered

Right, Jenni thought. *You are lying on top of me with your hand over my mouth, and I'm supposed to believe that you're not here to hurt me.* She struggled and tried to get him off of her, but to no avail. She stopped only when she had exhausted herself and knew that she couldn't overpower him.

After several long moments of stillness, he looked at her again. "Do you promise to not yell?"

She nodded. The hand immediately loosened but did not move away from her mouth. When he saw that she was not planning on screaming, he moved the hand several inches from her mouth but still close enough to put a stop to any attempts on her part to scream.

"Are you ready to listen? I promise you I am not here to hurt you. I know you have no reason to trust me, but Michael trusted me, so at least give me a chance to explain."

Michael may have trusted you but now he's dead.

"Fine," she said in a sullen tone.

He lifted himself off of her, but he stood between her and the doorway. She stood up.

"So, Billy Bob, I guess you got my e-mail. I should have figured it out when I saw your initials. I can't believe I was so stupid as not to know who BB was."

She saw herself looking at the business card she had found stuck in the antique TV safe. The name on the card had been William Robert Gindlesburger—BB. It

Chapter Sixteen

had been staring her in the face the whole time, and she hadn't seen it.

"Yes, I got your e-mail. I came because I was afraid you would get yourself in more trouble. I'm just trying to help you."

Jenni could only stare at him. His hair was falling in his bright blue eyes, which contrasted with his bronzed skin. She remembered the terror she felt as he chased her down the streets of Nassau. Her legs felt shaky. She sat down on the chair.

"I'm sorry that I scared you, but I needed to talk to you."

She glared at him. "You could have rung my doorbell the way other people do."

"I couldn't take the chance of you being able to get to the phone before I explained. I didn't want to get the police involved."

"I'll just bet you didn't."

"Stop looking at me that way. I'm not the bad guy here."

"You're the one that broke in my house. You're the one that chased me in Nassau. And I think you're the one that killed my husband. So, don't tell me that you're not the bad guy," she screamed at him.

"You're right about the first two, but not the last one. I didn't kill Michael. We were working together."

Chapter Seventeen

Dr. Gail Rinaldi was sitting dejectedly in the dingy little apartment that they jokingly called their love nest. She'd been so anxious to meet her lover, but she'd just received a phone call that plans had changed. There would be no rendezvous that night.

Her lover had laughed off the change of plans with the explanation that it was a problem when both people involved had high-pressured jobs that kept them busy, but Gail Rinaldi wasn't sure if that were the real reason.

Gail had thought she'd been in love in the past but now realized those had just been trial practices. This was the real thing for her, but she wasn't as confident about her lover.

Gail Rinaldi had compromised her personal and professional ethics to try and help out her lover, but now that she'd done it, she felt as if she'd been discarded. Broken appointments, missed dates, lousy excuses. She

Shattered

felt as if she'd been used but knew she had no one to blame but herself. She'd known it was wrong, but her lover had been so desperate and had promised they would go away together if Gail would just help with the little matter of Jenni Hamilton.

Against her better judgement she'd done what her lover had asked. Gail had never wanted to hurt Jenni, and she hadn't done anything that would hurt her in the long run. All she'd really done was to plant some suggestions to stop worrying about her husband and get on with her life. That was actually good advice for Jenni Hamilton. So, if you looked at it that way, Gail hadn't done anything that wrong. She'd had a court order to keep Jenni hospitalized. They couldn't prove that she'd done anything illegal.

She didn't want to think about her lover's involvement in Michael's death. The explanation to her had been that they just wanted Jenni to feel better. Gail had decided to accept that explanation without any questions.

Chapter Eighteen

Billy Bob pushed his shoulder-length brown hair out of his eyes and smiled at Jenni. She did not return the smile. She tried to stop trembling but couldn't.

"I'm an agent for the FBI, and Michael was helping me with an investigation."

Jenni gaped at him. This was not one of the many ideas that had occurred to her over the last few months. The man standing before her looked like an aging hippie, not a federal agent.

Billy Bob waited, but when she didn't say anything, he continued, "We had reason to believe that someone at Marshall Corporation was importing drugs along with their shipments of legitimate supplies. Michael was trying to help us find out who it was."

She sat on the chair trying to absorb the things he was saying. "So, you recruited Michael?"

Shattered

"Not exactly. He's the one that came to us. He made regular spot checks of inventory to make sure that the company wasn't being cheated by their suppliers or the employees. During one of the spot checks, he came across a drug shipment. He immediately contacted us and agreed to help us."

Tears threatened. That sounded just like Michael to be that meticulous. Of course he would have contacted the police and offered to help never thinking of his own safety.

"Why didn't you protect him?" she asked bitterly.

"I'm not going to sit here and make excuses. We—let me change that—*I* didn't do my job. I know that. I take full responsibility. We were not aware of the local investigation dealing with the embezzlement. If we had been, well, we could have done something to help, but I guess it doesn't matter now."

Anger flashed in Jenni's eyes. "It matters to me. Why didn't you come forward and clear his name when he was arrested?"

"We would have helped him but . . ." His voice drifted off, and he broke eye contact with her. "We didn't want to hamper the investigation."

His answer infuriated her. "So, who was it?"

"Michael had it narrowed down, but we didn't know for sure."

"Well, who did he suspect?"

"I can't give you that information."

Chapter Eighteen

Jenni jumped up. "Excuse me. My husband is dead and you won't tell me who is responsible."

He was adamant. "That would be unconscionable since we have no proof. It would only make the situation worse."

Jenni screamed in frustration. "I have a right to know!"

Billy Bob flinched but didn't look away. He spoke softly. "I don't disagree, but we don't know, and I'm not going to give you names of people that could be innocent. I've already ruined enough people's lives as it is."

She sagged, her energy depleted. She spoke in a listless voice, barely above a whisper. "I knew he hadn't done those things. I knew it."

"That's not necessarily true."

Jenni looked up confusion clouding her eyes. "Excuse me?"

"The fact that he was helping us does not necessarily preclude the fact that he could have been embezzling money from the company or that he'd plan to flee the country. And in some ways, it might even explain it."

Jenni glared at Billy Bob but finally asked, "Why?"

He gave a shrug and shifted uncomfortably from one foot to another. "If he thought the company might go under, it might have been the catalyst to steal the money. To be sure that you would be provided for."

She shook her head vehemently. "I don't believe that. We have plenty of money. Michael was good at investing. He could have retired whenever he had chosen to."

Shattered

She started to say something about Jasmine then caught herself. She would not endanger Jasmine DuPree or her son. Now he was the one that began pacing. Jenni watched but didn't interrupt his pacing. After several minutes, he looked at her and sat back down on the bed.

"You're right. I don't believe it either. What I was telling you was the company line. That's the official explanation, but I never bought into it. Anyone who knew Michael for more than a few days would know that he wouldn't have done it for any reason."

Jenni gave him a smile. Her first real smile in a long time. Finally someone agreed with her. "So, what's happening with the investigation?"

He frowned. "Nothing. The investigation was closed."

"Closed?" She felt as if she'd been punched in the stomach.

"I fought it but my bosses voted me down. I tried to tell them that someone had murdered Michael, and it was our obligation to find out who. They refused to listen."

"That's why you didn't want me to call the police?"

"Exactly. They wouldn't be happy to know we were in contact with each other."

"Why did you follow me to the Bahamas? How did you even know I was in the Bahamas?"

He looked uncomfortable. "I thought you might be in danger. I felt I owed it to Michael to keep you safe. I was there on my own time. It wasn't official."

Chapter Eighteen

"I won't let them get away with murdering Michael."

"They already have." Billy Bob's eyes were sad as he spoke. "I'm not happy about it either, but there is nothing to be done. I only came here tonight to give you some peace of mind. I wanted you to know how much Michael loved you. At every meeting, he would insist that your safety had to be the number one priority. I didn't want you spending the rest of your life thinking that he betrayed you."

Jenni gave him a hateful stare. She twisted her wedding ring. "You needn't have worried yourself. I knew he loved me and would never do the things that everyone was saying."

"I wasn't the one saying those things," Billy Bob reminded her, not that he thought it would do any good. He didn't blame her at all for being angry.

"Maybe not, but you could have set the record straight and you didn't."

"It wasn't my decision."

"So, that's it. It's just all done, just like that."

The comment gave Billy Bob hope that she would stop pursuing the truth.

"I think it's best. For your own safety." The second it came out of his mouth he knew it was a mistake, but he couldn't take it back.

Jenni spun around and faced him, hands on her hips. "Is that what you think? That I'm worried about my own safety? You couldn't be more wrong. What I care about is clearing Michael's name." Her voice began cracking. "He gave me so much and I gave him so little, but I will give him back his reputation even if it kills me."

"That's what I'm afraid of. I promised Michael that you would be safe. He wouldn't want you to do this."

"Well, I absolve you of that promise. Now, just leave me alone. I will figure this out on my own."

"Can't you see how dangerous that would be?" Billy Bob let his frustration show.

"Can't you see that I don't care?" She glowered back at him.

They were at an impasse. Each glared at the other. Jenni wouldn't change her mind.

Finally Billy Bob broke the silence. "What is it that you think you're going to do that a group of professional law enforcement officers couldn't do?"

"I don't know, but I'll figure something out." She paced around the office for a moment. "It's time for you to go. Thank you for telling me that Michael loved me."

"What are you going to do?"

She ignored him and waited for him to walk to the door. He did. She followed him down the steps and walked to the front door and opened that one for him. He stood facing her and repeated the question.

"What are you going to do?"

"It's none of your business. You are not my keeper. Go back to your job and forget all about it."

Chapter Eighteen

He ignored her outburst and instead looked at his watch. "It's too late to come up with an idea tonight. We can talk tomorrow."

"Why?"

"So you won't get yourself killed."

"I'll be fine."

He brushed his long hair away from his face. "I'm trying to tell you that I will help you."

"No, it will jeopardize your job."

"It doesn't matter. I'm not going to let you do this alone."

She relented. "Fine. When do you want to meet?"

"I can't come until later in the day, after I'm done working."

"Fine. We can meet here. I'll cook dinner."

"I'll be here with bells on." That earned him a small tight smile, which was more than he had any right to expect. It was only after he was gone that she realized she should have asked to see an ID.

Jenni wandered through the house double-checking the locks on the doors and windows. She would be calling a security company to install a security system as soon as possible. There was no way someone was going to walk into her house like that again. FBI or not, they would have to answer to the police for breaking into her house.

Too jumpy to go back upstairs she laid down on the couch. She tossed and turned willing herself to go to sleep. It didn't happen.

Shattered

Billy Bob had scared her when he jumped out at her in the dark, but the things he'd told her were more terrifying. Now she knew there were people out there who would stop at nothing to keep the truth hidden.

Chapter Nineteen

Jenni looked at the clock on the wall. She'd slept for less than three hours, and her body felt it. She stood and stretched trying to loosen the knots she felt. Her body was stiff and sore from sleeping on the sofa.

She looked around the room and wondered again how Billy Bob had gotten into her house. She hadn't asked him the previous night. She'd been too shocked to think straight then. She inspected the doors and the windows and came to the conclusion that he must have been able to pick the locks. She would have thought that was illegal even for an FBI agent. He could have just called her, and she would have been willing to listen to him.

As she showered, she allowed her mind free rein to consider options and ideas of what her next move would be, with or without Billy Bob. She wasn't sure she wanted

Shattered

him to jeopardize his job for her. She didn't want to put any one else but herself in danger.

When she was finished showering, she dressed and went to the kitchen to make coffee. She jumped when the doorbell rang. Maybe, Billy Bob had decided to come earlier than planned. She walked to her living room window and looked out her window. Carmen's car sat in the driveway.

She went to answer the door. She already felt guilty about not contacting Carmen since she'd been home. She'd called other friends but not Carmen. She couldn't verbalize what the problem was. She loved Carmen but something felt wrong. Maybe, she was still mad at Roberto for helping to get her hospitalized.

She opened the door. Instead of Carmen, Roberto was standing on her porch. Her stomach lurched but she managed to smile. "Hi. When I looked out the window, I thought it was Carmen."

"No, just me." He cleared his throat nervously. "Can I come in?"

"Oh, sure." Jenni moved away from the door and motioned him in. "I was just surprised to see you."

"I can come back another time if you're busy."

"What do I have to do that would keep me busy?" They both stood looking at each other. She smiled. "Sorry, just feeling sorry for myself. Would you like coffee?"

"I don't want you to go to any bother," he said it formally and stiffly.

Chapter Nineteen

She led the way to the kitchen. "It's no bother, it's already made." She was grateful to have something to do with her hands. She wondered how Roberto knew she was back. After a few moments, she turned from the coffee machine and looked at Roberto. "Is there something wrong?"

He gave her a cheerful smile that felt false to her. "No, no. Not at all. I just wanted to come by and check on you. I haven't seen much of you since . . . well since Michael died. Your mom called and told us you were back, so I just wanted to see how you were."

She felt tears but ignored them. "I'm OK. I'm getting better every day."

"I know you must be angry with me." He took a sip of coffee.

Jenni looked at him, but he wouldn't meet her eyes. She waited.

He finally met her eyes and smiled at her. "I only did what I thought was best."

"Why did you think that was best?" she asked softly. She didn't want a fight. She was tired of confrontation. She wanted her friend back.

He ignored her question and asked one of his own. "So, I guess you believe that Michael did what they're saying?"

She couldn't meet his eyes. "I suppose." She looked up. "You do, right?"

Shattered

"So, you're done trying to prove that he didn't do it." It sounded more like a question than a statement. She noticed he hadn't answered her question. She thought of telling him the truth but knew that she couldn't trust him. She gave him a nod.

"Good. I don't want anything happening to you." He smiled but still looked as if he had more to say.

"What's that supposed to mean, Roberto?" Jenni asked sharply. "I thought all of that was just a delusion. Now, you sit here telling me that you don't want anything to happen to me. What do you know that I don't know?" she demanded.

"Nothing. That's not what I meant." He looked flustered, as if she'd caught him in a lie. He stood up from the counter and was backing away to stop the barrage of questions.

"I want to know what you know. You owe that to Michael." She took a few steps forward. He backed off further.

"You're overreacting, Jenni. That is not what I meant."

"Yeah, I heard you the first time. Now, tell me the truth." Their eyes met and she knew he knew something. She could feel it. She decided to take the risk and trust him.

"I already know part of it. So, you might as well tell me what you know."

He kept shaking his head and moving away from her. "I don't know what you're talking about, Jenni. I

Chapter Nineteen

think you are still confused. Maybe you should talk to that doctor some more."

"I'll just bet you do, Roberto," she said bitterly. She sat back down at the counter and choked back sobs. He was involved. How could he betray his closest friend?

"I hope you will forgive me for my role in sending you to the hospital. I only did what I thought was best for you. I truly was worried about you, Jenni. I just wanted to keep you safe."

She nodded. "Why would you think I wasn't safe, Robbie?"

His eyes widened at the question and his face turned ruddy. "I . . . I . . . I just meant . . . Well, what I mean . . . You know. You were distraught. You had just lost Michael. I was afraid for you."

He jumped up and took his coffee cup to the sink. He busied himself washing out the cup. Jenni watched. He was hiding something. She was sure that he knew more about whatever was happening.

He turned back to her. "I must go. Time to get to work."

"No, Roberto. I want to know what is going on."

He looked at her for a moment. Then moved toward her. He wrapped her in a big bear hug. She could barely breathe. His mouth moved to her ear. He whispered fiercely, "No, no. You need to stay alive. Forget about all of this. Michael is gone. I don't want anything to happen to you."

Shattered

He let go of her as quickly as he hugged her and was gone before she could respond to the things he'd said. She looked at the clock. She wasn't done with Roberto, but she would wait until Carmen was at the office. He wouldn't be able to lie to Carmen. Jenni was too wired to just sit at home. She threw some chicken, rice, and salsa in the crockpot for dinner that night with Billy Bob and walked out to her car.

She sat at the crossroads by her house drumming the steering wheel with her fingers deciding where to go. She made a right turn away from town and the decision was made. She hadn't been back to the cemetery since the day she'd buried Michael.

As she walked past the other plots, it was hard not to miss all the beautiful flower arrangements and plants that adorned them. She looked at the marker and her eyes teared up as she read his name. She felt a twinge of guilt for not coming sooner, but both she and Michael had discussed many times about visiting gravesites. It didn't make sense. The only thing in the ground was a body, not the spirit of the loved one.

With that thought, she realized how foolish she'd been to come here. Wherever Michael was, he wasn't here in the ground. She didn't care what others were saying about him. He was a good man. He was a Christian and his spirit was in heaven.

She felt a peace descend on her. She hadn't thought of that before. She'd been in too much pain herself.

Chapter Nineteen

Michael was OK now. He was in the arms of God. He was safe.

Happy tears flowed for the first time. Michael was in heaven. She could stop worrying about him. She sank to the grass and wept.

"Oh, Michael. I didn't know I would have to live without you, but I'm glad you're in heaven. It must be wonderful there."

She lifted her face to the sky. She felt the warmth of the sun. She wasn't OK yet, but she would be someday when she was able to start healing, but she couldn't start healing until the people that were responsible for Michael's death were punished.

She stood up and turned to leave and almost jumped out of her skin when she saw a man standing several feet behind her. He stood watching her. When she gave a small scream of fright, he smiled reassuringly at her.

"Sorry, I didn't mean to scare you." He spoke softly in an unassuming manner.

Jenni began walking back to her car making a wide berth around the man still standing in the same spot as when she found him.

"I know how that is. I couldn't come here for months after my wife died. The first time is the hardest. Is your loss recent?"

Jenni did not want to stand here discussing Michael's death with a stranger, but she didn't want to be rude either. "I guess you could say that," she said quietly but continued to walk to her car to discourage the man from more conversation. He said nothing else. Once in the car, Jenni watched him walk up to a grave and kneel beside it. She gave a sigh of relief; she didn't like being around strangers anymore. It was hard to know whom to trust.

She drove to Roberto's law office, which was located at a popular mall. She opened the door and walked in. Carmen's desk was empty, but the door to Roberto's office was open. She walked in. Roberto and Carmen were in the middle of a kiss.

They broke apart. Carmen gave her a smile. "I wondered when you were going to tell me you were back."

Jenni wasn't in the mood for chitchat. She looked at Roberto. "We need to finish our conversation."

Carmen looked taken aback by Jenni's tone.

"Did Roberto tell you he stopped at my house this morning?"

Carmen's long black hair moved with her head as she shook it. She looked at Roberto with surprise. "No."

Roberto hadn't said anything yet. He looked back and forth between the two women and gave a little shrug of surrender. He held a hand to his mouth to quiet them. He motioned for them to follow him out of the office and then hung a sign on the door that said Closed. He locked the door. No one spoke as they followed him to the mall food court.

Chapter Nineteen

"Let's go get something to drink." He smiled reassuringly at both women.

"I think we need privacy, Robbie." Carmen looked terrified.

"I agree. That's why we're here. I'll go get lunch."

The food court was full of shoppers taking a break. Carmen and Jenni found a table and sat down, still not speaking. They looked at each other. Both tried to smile for the other but failed.

Roberto walked up with a tray laden with food and a big smile on his face. He talked softly. "You need to both stop looking at me like that. I haven't done anything wrong. We want this to look like we are having a friendly lunch, so smile. Comprende?" Both women nodded and smiled but looked at him as if he'd gone crazy.

He passed out food and the smile never left his face. He sat down. "Remember, don't look upset. We are just three friends having lunch. Do you understand?"

Carmen smiled but her eyes betrayed her feelings. "Why?"

Roberto spoke softly. "I found recording devices in the office."

Comprehension dawned. Jenni said, "You mean 'bugs'"?

He nodded and took a big bite of his hot dog. He gave them a meaningful glance and both women grabbed their food and took a bite. Carmen's voice was shrill. "What do you mean? Recording devices?"

Shattered

Roberto grabbed her hands. "You need to stay calm, Carmen. This is important. Cut the theatrics, just this one time, baby."

"OK," she said softly.

"Who put the recording devices in the office, Roberto?" asked Jenni.

"I don't know. I'm sorry I upset you this morning, Jenni. I just needed to make sure you really had given up this idea to find Michael's murderer. I want you to be safe. I wasn't able to keep Michael safe." His voice broke on the last words.

Carmen looked shell-shocked. "Michael's murderer? I thought you believed he killed himself."

Roberto reached for his soft drink. He took hold of Carmen's hand and smiled lovingly at his wife. He turned back to Jenni. "Now, I've got you all worked up again. My visit made you more suspicious."

"No, it didn't. I found information that made me believe in Michael's innocence."

"Like what?"

"I caught people in lies." She wasn't sure how much to say. "What do you know?"

"Not a lot. I knew something was going on with Michael. He wouldn't tell me what. And then some strange things happened."

"What kind of things?" Carmen asked before Jenni could.

Chapter Nineteen

"I found a recording device in the office. Someone followed me a few times. I went to the police, and they assured me they had not bugged my office. It's illegal to do that in an attorney's office. I haven't found anymore since then, but you never know."

Maybe Michael had been the one that placed it there; perhaps he was suspicious of Roberto. Jenni kept that thought to herself. "Did you talk to Michael about it?" Jenni asked knowing that the two men usually shared everything.

"Yes, he got a funny look on his face, but when I asked him why, he said he would tell me as soon as he could. I'd already known something was going on. Several times he'd meet with me and then tell me he had to leave but asked if I would cover for him if anyone asked me where he was."

"Did you think he might be having an affair?" Carmen asked, her accent thickening with each word.

"I asked him that and he said no. I believed him. He said he was having a few problems and that he would tell me when he could. I told him I would help him, and he just said covering for him would be enough."

"Did you ever need to do that?" Jenni asked and then lifted up the cup to take a sip from the straw.

Roberto thought for a moment. "Actually, there were a few times when I was with Nicholas and he asked me what Michael and I had done the night before. I'd make up something, like doing work on the house or going to a game."

"Anybody else?"

"Well, once when I was at Marshall, Annie Meyers asked me what I'd done the night before, and without thinking I told her that Carmen and I had gone to see a movie. Then, I remembered that Michael had asked me to cover for him that night, so I added that Michael and you had gone with us. She didn't seem all that interested, just making conversation before the meeting."

Roberto looked at Jenni. She didn't know what to do or what to believe. She had to make a decision to trust him now and tell him the truth or believe that he'd helped someone hurt Michael. She took a deep breath and hoped she would make the right decision.

The man sat in the mall and watched the three of them talking. He cursed; there was no way he could hear what they were saying with this many people in the food court. He didn't dare get any closer. He didn't want Jenni to see him. He'd known she wouldn't be able to wait for him. He only hoped she wasn't making the situation worse by talking to Carmen and Roberto about the things he'd told her last night.

He finally gave up and went to sit in his car to wait for Jenni. No sense taking the chance that she would see him. His bosses weren't going to be happy with the fact that his report would basically be a non-report. She had lunch with friends and she may or may not have

Chapter Nineteen

told them of her suspicions. He had no reason to think she was telling them. None of them looked overly excited or worried. No doubt just three friends having a quick lunch.

He watched Jenni as she unlocked her car. She didn't seem to be agitated. He breathed a sigh of relief, maybe he would just tell his bosses that she'd gone to lunch but nothing remarkable happened. He followed leaving plenty of space between them. He watched as she went to the bank and the post office. Her third stop was home.

He parked down the block from Jenni's house. He hit the send button on his cell phone and waited. He was just about to give up when he finally heard, "Hello."

"It's me. She's at home now. She went to the mall and had lunch with Carmen and Roberto, then to the bank and the post office."

"What did she talk about with them?"

He considered lying but decided against it. "I don't know."

"Why not?" came the scream from the other end of the phone. "With all that expensive equipment you've got."

"They sat in the food court. It was too noisy unless I took the chance to get closer."

He could hear his boss pounding on his desk. "I need to know what she's planning. Father isn't going to be happy about this."

"Hopefully, I'll be able to find out tonight."

Shattered

"Well, you keep doing what you're doing. I'll put someone else on it too."

"I can handle it. I don't need help."

"But that's my decision, don't you think?"

He could hear the anger in his boss's voice. "Of course. I just meant that I can handle it, but it's no problem if you wanted to bring someone else in."

"Thanks for your permission." The connection was broken with neither person saying good-bye.

Jenni looked at the clock on the wall. It would be a few more hours before Billy Bob arrived. She was too antsy to sit still, so she went upstairs to pack more of Michael's things. When she had a full trash bag, she walked it out to the garage. Her neighbor was outside gardening. Jenni walked over and said hello.

Nellie was much older than her and had been a widow for as long as Michael and Jenni had lived in the house.

"Hi, Nellie."

"Oh, thank goodness, you're here, Jenni. I was just trying to decide what to do."

The term "Nervous Nellie" must have been invented after having met Jenni's neighbor. Every problem was a crisis. Jenni wondered what the current crisis was, a mealy bug or a mite on one of her beloved roses.

"What's the problem, Nellie?"

"There's been a car sitting down the block off and on all day. He's back now. I was thinking about calling the police but after the last time. I thought someone

Chapter Nineteen

was trying to break in and it was just that silly tree limb. Well, let's just say I don't want to feel that foolish again."

"They're probably just visiting with someone."

"Oh no, he's in the car. I can see him from my upstairs window."

A thought nudged its way into Jenni's brain. "Are you sure there is someone in the car?" Jenni stretched her neck but couldn't see a car.

"Absolutely." Nellie nodded vigorously to emphasize her point. Then added sheepishly, "I used my binoculars."

Jenni licked her lips.

"You know, Nellie. I think you should call the police. But could you do me a favor and don't mention my name when you do?" Jenni knew that sounded odd. "You know with the trouble with Michael, I'd just as soon stay out of it."

Nellie patted her hand bravely. "Of course, dear. You go on back into the house, and I'll take care of it myself."

Jenni knew she had to be quick. She had to leave while the man down the block was being distracted by the police. She rushed upstairs and looked around her room. She needed to take something with her, but she just didn't know what to choose. She shoved a few clothes in a suitcase and looked around. Her eyes fell on her wedding album on the nightstand. She put that in the bag with the clothes, grabbed her purse, and started out to the car, but she stopped dead in her tracks.

Shattered

She could easily be traced by driving the car. Not to mention if Roberto was correct about his office being bugged, it wasn't out of the realm of possibility that her car and her house were both being bugged somehow. She went back to the front window and saw that indeed the police were driving slowly past her house toward the unwanted car.

Back in the kitchen, she looked around, expecting someone to tell her what to do. Her eyes landed on the crock pot. She walked back and unplugged it. She walked through her backyard and opened the gate that she shared with her neighbors.

Their dog, the one that was always barking, ran to greet her, his tail wagging the rest of his body. She knew they wouldn't be home since they both worked, but she knew where their house key was, as they knew where hers was in case of an emergency.

Once safely in their house, she sat letting her racing heart normalize for a few moments. She wanted a clear head. No one knew where she was unless they had cameras hidden in her bushes, which even she thought was unlikely. She sat there wondering what to do.

She reached for the phone.

Chapter Twenty

After a cab drive and several bus changes, Jenni found herself sitting in a cheap motel on the outskirts of town reading directions from the box of a hair-coloring product. As much as she liked her new hair color, it would have to go. She didn't want anyone to recognize her. She had chosen blonde this time.

She turned the TV on while waiting for the color to process. The news had begun. Maybe listening to the troubles of others would make her feel better. It didn't work.

The announcer blared, "Breaking news. This just in; there is a house fire raging in the exclusive area of Brandywine." She looked up; that was where she lived. The TV broke to a vapid-looking news reporter that showed firefighters working diligently in the background. She gasped as she looked at her house in flames.

Shattered

Jenni felt her heart break yet again. That house had been their dream home and now it was gone. It was like killing Michael all over again. She sat there watching her house burn. When they went back to regular programming, she curled up in a ball on the bed. Trying to get hold of herself but it was suddenly all too much.

After a long time, she prayed. *Dear God, help me. I don't know what to do. Help me.* After a few minutes, she felt calmness descend. She sat up and took several deep breaths. Logic replaced emotion. She would get to the bottom or die trying.

She looked over at the TV that was still blaring, reminding her of the fire and her house. She took a deep breath. She refused to let her emotions take over. The house may have been a symbol of her and Michael's past, but it was still just a possession. They couldn't burn away her memories. They couldn't take their love away.

She sat on the bed pondering what her next move would be. She would never be safe until the truth came out. She knew that now. This had to end one way or another.

Jenni's eyes fell on the box of hair coloring. She jumped up with a yelp. She'd forgotten about the hair coloring on her head. She ran to the bathroom and stuck her head under the sink. She watched the red-colored water swirl down the pipe until it turned pink and finally ran clear. She put a towel around her hair. She'd thought the water should have been yellow-colored. She had no idea what color her hair would end up.

Chapter Twenty

Jenni walked to the bed and lay down. Her jumbled thoughts bounced around inside her head. She didn't try to stop them. She let her mind work without any interference from her.

Nicholas might be behind the whole thing, but it would do no good to go confront Nicholas Peyton. He would just laugh at her accusations and talk her mother into putting her back in the hospital. The truth was that she had no proof against him or anyone else for that matter and no way to get proof. She sighed in frustration. If she confronted Nicholas, he would find a way to put her back in Dr. Rinaldi's clinic, and she might never get out.

She could go confront Roberto, but she didn't want him to be involved. Yes, he had helped to have her hospitalized against her will, but she wanted to believe that he'd done it for her. Besides, if she wrongly accused him, that would be the end of their friendship.

There was only one person that she knew was definitely involved. That was Dr. Gail Rinaldi. Dr. Rinaldi was the key to finding out the truth. Gail Rinaldi was involved. Jenni just didn't know how or why she was involved, only that she was involved.

Dr. Rinaldi was the key. She'd used hypnosis and drugged her with only one goal in mind. She wanted Jenni to believe the lies about Michael. She'd never tried to get Jenni to discuss any of the feelings about Michael and his death. Every session was about Jenni accepting that Michael had betrayed her.

Shattered

Why had Gail Rinaldi done it? Someone had probably paid her a lot of money to brainwash Jenni into believing that Michael was guilty, but who was the question.

Jenni needed more information about Dr. Rinaldi, but how was she supposed to do that? Then it came to her; Billy Bob would be able to find out more information about her. Unfortunately the only way she knew to contact him was through the e-mail program that had burned up with the rest of her house.

She reached for the phone book. After finding the number, she dialed and it rang only twice before an official sounding voice said, "Offices of the Federal Bureau of Investigation."

"I need to speak to someone that works there, but I'm not sure what department."

"Give me his name and I'll check for you."

"Thanks. His name is William Robert Gindlesburger."

"Hold on while I check. What is your name, please?" Jenni was positive that the woman had an odd tone in her voice.

"Why do you need to know that?"

"So I can tell him who's calling when I connect, ma'am."

"Oh, well . . ." Jenni stumbled around trying to think of a response. "I'd rather not say."

There was a long pause. "Just one moment, please."

Chapter Twenty

Jenni's instincts told her to hang up, but she needed Billy Bob's help. She waited for what seemed like an eternity before a man's voice answered—but not Billy Bob. "Hello, Can I help you?"

"You're not Billy Bob."

"No, I'm not. I'm his supervisor. He's not available, but I'll be glad to take a message"

"I need to talk him. It's personal." Panic slipped into her voice.

"I understand and I'll be gla—"

"Never mind." Jenni hung up. The tiny room suddenly felt claustrophobic. She needed fresh air. She jumped up and checked her hair in the mirror. Her hair was the shade of blonde that the box had promised. She ran her fingers through it a few times and left the hotel room. She walked across the street to a small diner, not because she was particularly hungry, but it gave her a place to go.

She ordered a cheeseburger and sat trying to figure out another way to reach Billy Bob. She didn't want to get him in trouble with his bosses by letting them know that the two of them were still in contact with each other.

Sirens and screeching tires drew her attention back to the motel. A car pulled into the parking lot and two men jumped out of the car. They wore jackets with the letters F.B.I. emblazoned on them. She sat immobilized, stupidly watching them as if it were on a TV screen and not across the street storming her motel room.

Shattered

She sat and watched them knock several times on her door. When nothing happened, one of the men jogged over to the motel office. The other stood guarding her door.

The man walked out of the motel's registration office and over to another man still standing by the car. The men drew guns. The guns brought her back to reality. She jumped up, spilling her water. Several patrons looked at her as the glass shattered on the floor.

She bent down to clean it. The waitress was just bringing her food to the table.

"Don't worry. I'll clean that up."

"Oh, thanks." Jenni reached in her purse and pulled out a twenty. "I'm sorry but I have to leave. Here's money for the food and a tip for you. Sorry about the mess."

"That's OK."

Jenni glanced out the window one last time and saw the men coming out of her room. It looked as if they were looking directly at her from across the street. She couldn't walk out that front door and let them see her. She looked at the waitress and whispered, "Is there a back door?"

Comprehension dawned in the waitress's eyes. Jenni was sure that she would grab her and start screaming. Jenni pulled out another twenty. The waitress thought for a moment and then nodded. "Follow me."

Jenni said, "Thanks."

Chapter Twenty

She hurried to the back of the restaurant. This was crazy. Why was she hiding from the F.B.I.? She hadn't done anything wrong. She had been the one that contacted them. She'd wanted Billy Bob to help her, and now she was running from him. She felt absurd for running away, but it felt like the right thing to do. She shivered as she thought of the guns they'd held in their hands. Perhaps, they thought she was involved with the drugs that Billy Bob had told her about, and they were after her now.

The two agents stood by their car. The shorter man looked at the tall black man standing next to him. "It looks like we just missed her, Bill."

Billy Bob shook his head in confusion. "I wonder why she left. She's the one that called us."

"True, but she probably didn't expect us to come riding in like the Calvary," the shorter man said. "She must be freaking if she knows about her house. I know I would be."

Billy Bob agreed. "With good reason. I just wished she'd let us help. We can keep her safe."

"At least we know she has blonde hair now. We can have the computer artist change this picture, put out an APB, and hopefully find her before they do."

"Too bad we don't know who *they* are. It would be a lot easier to protect her if we did."

The men got in their car and went back to report that it looked as if Jenni Hamilton was officially on the

Shattered

run again. Before they left the location, they put in a call to have the motel watched, just in case Jenni came back to the room. The two agents didn't think that was likely, but it was always good to cover all the bases.

Jenni went in to the first store she saw and bought a few things, not out of any pressing need, but to give her something normal to do. After that, she found an ATM machine and took out the daily limit on each of the three ATM cards that she had. That would give her enough money for a few days.

She needed a car, but in order to rent a car she would have to use her credit card. She thought that she remembered that the police and the FBI could monitor someone's credit card activity. She pondered her dilemma and knew that she had few choices, her mother or Carmen and Roberto. And since her mother might still think she was crazy that left one choice.

She wasn't sure what Roberto's role was in all of this, but it was hard for her to believe that he would have done anything to hurt Michael, and she'd already trusted Roberto enough to tell him what she had learned from Billy Bob.

She walked until she found a payphone.

Jenni swallowed hard when she heard Carmen's voice. "It's me."

"Are you OK? We were watching the news and saw your house. We've been scared to death since we heard about your house."

Chapter Twenty

"I'm OK, but I need a car."

"You can borrow one of ours. Hold on a minute, someone's at the door. Robbie Jr., get the door."

Jenni heard male voices and then heard Carmen's voice get louder, and she said, "FBI." Jenni quietly hung up the phone.

The two men stood in Carmen's living room. The tall black man introduced himself. "I'm Agent William Gindlesburger, and this is Agent Stanley Johns. We need to talk to you and your husband about Jenni Hamilton."

Carmen nodded and told them to hold on a moment. She quietly put the phone down. Roberto was already walking down the steps. Roberto looked at the men and knew immediately that they were police officers of some sort. He shook hands with the men as they introduced themselves.

Billy Bob spoke. "Let's get right down to business. We are worried about Jenni Hamilton's safety."

"So are we," Carmen jumped in. She hadn't learned to be as cautious as Roberto. He gave her a look. She went to the kids and shooed them upstairs.

"Could I see some ID, please?" Roberto asked.

Both men pulled out their wallets and handed them to Roberto. He slowly looked at each of them and at the men that stood in front of him. "You don't mind if I call the offices and check on the two of you, do you?"

"Not at all, the number is 555–76 . . ."

Shattered

Roberto held up his hand and stopped Stanley. "That's OK. I'll look it up myself."

Roberto proceeded to the phone book and talked to two different people before he was satisfied that the two men were indeed FBI agents. He motioned for them to sit down. After everyone was seated, Roberto smiled at them.

"Sorry about that, but I needed to be sure that you were some of the good guys. Now, I want to help you, but first I need a few questions answered."

Chapter Twenty-one

Jenni thought about it as she waited for the bus. She couldn't borrow a car, couldn't rent a car. That only left one option, she would have to steal a car. She didn't know how, but necessity was the mother of invention, or so they said.

Once on the bus, she realized just how exhausted she was. She must be losing her mind if she actually was thinking of a stealing a car. She didn't even need a car. She had nowhere to go. What she needed was a place to rest. The bus stopped at a mall and Jenni got off and began to walk. She went into the first hotel she saw. She ran into a snag when she wanted to pay cash instead of using a credit card, but they finally agreed, and she had her room without having to show an ID or registering under her own name.

Once in the room, she threw herself on the large king-size bed. She was drained physically and emotionally. After a short nap, she ordered from room service. She heard the knock of room service. She opened the door to the smiling face of a young man.

"Room service."

"How are you?"

"Fine. And yourself?"

"Having a bit of a bad day, if you know what I mean."

"I sure do. Been there a couple of times myself. Anything I can help you with?"

The question made her think. An idea began to form. "I don't know. Maybe so. I lost my credit cards, which means I can't rent a car, but I need a car for the next few days. You know anyone that might be willing to lend me car? I'd be glad to pay—a lot of money."

She saw a glint of interest in his eyes. "How much are you talking about?"

"I don't know, maybe five hundred dollars to start with. And if I need the car for more than two days, I'll give you another five hundred when I return it."

A smile broke out on his face. He held out his hand to shake. "You've got a deal. I own a Ford Escort. It's not pretty but it's dependable. I can take the bus to work and back for two days."

"Great. When can I get the car?"

He reached in his pocket and held out the keys. She went to her purse and handed him five hundred dollars. And their transaction was completed. With that problem

Chapter Twenty-one

taken care of, she sat down to her meal and enjoyed the club sandwich. The bacon was cooked to perfection.

She went to the phone book and looked for Gail Rinaldi in the white pages and in the yellow pages under Doctors. No luck. She tapped her fingers on the desk. She called down to the front desk.

"Is it possible to get access to the Internet from my room?"

"Yes, but you have to have your own laptop," the polite voice explained.

"Oh, I don't have one."

"We have several in the conference center if you want to use one."

"That would be great."

Jenni walked to the front desk, and they promptly took her to the conference center. She didn't even have to log on under her name. It was already set up to their networks.

She typed in Doctor Gail Rinaldi and waited. Magically, several different listings popped on the page. The first one was an article that Dr. Rinaldi had written about hypnosis. The second was another article about the same topic. The third was an article written about her in the local paper.

She read several more articles about Dr. Rinaldi and her clinic. Apparently, Dr. Rinaldi was a very respected psychiatrist. Her clinic attracted the rich and famous. It didn't make sense to Jenni. Why would a doctor with

Shattered

that kind of reputation get involved in illegal activities? Jenni didn't have an answer for that.

As Jenni read the articles, she saw what she was looking for, the name of Dr. Rinaldi's clinic, Better Times Clinic. She rolled her eyes as she continued reading. It talked about a holistic approach to good health and well-being. Jenni wondered sarcastically to herself if the doctor's clients would be interested in knowing that included drugs being given without consent.

The article didn't give an address for the Better Times Medical Clinic, but it only took a few seconds to find one using the Internet. She wrote down the address and phone number.

She went to another web site and had it draw a map from her hotel to the Better Times Clinic. It wasn't that far. Jenni looked at her watch. It was already past seven o'clock. Dr. Rinaldi probably wasn't even at the clinic so late, but it couldn't hurt to try.

Once she was back in her room, Jenni dialed the number and asked for Dr. Rinaldi. When she was asked for her name, she told them the truth. She figured that would get her through to Dr. Rinaldi, if she were in the building. It did.

"Hello."

"Hello, Dr. Rinaldi."

"Jenni, is that you? Are you OK? Where are you?"

The woman's monotone was gone now. She sounded panicked. Jenni smiled. That was exactly what she wanted.

Chapter Twenty-one

"Yes, it's me. How are you, Dr. Rinaldi? I just wanted to give you an opportunity to tell me the truth before I go to the newspapers and tell them what you did to me at your clinic."

Jenni heard a gasp, but Dr. Rinaldi said nothing for a few moments. Finally she said in a much calmer tone, "I'm not sure what you mean, Jenni. I know you must be upset about your house. If you come over, we can talk about it."

"Will we talk about it before or after you drug me, Dr. Rinaldi?"

"Now, Jenni. I didn't do anything that wasn't for your own good."

"I think the newspapers will be very interested in my story."

"You are a very disturbed woman, Jenni. I only want to help you. I haven't done anything illegal."

"Well, if you want to help me, then why don't you tell me who you are working for? Who paid you to drug me and then brainwash me into believing that my husband was a thief?"

Again, there was no response for several moments. When Dr. Rinaldi did speak it was in that monotone that Jenni had grown to hate. "Why don't you come over here, and we can talk this out?"

"You know, that sounds like a very good idea. I think I might just do that." Jenni looked at her watch. "It will take me about forty minutes to get there. See you then." Jenni hung up before Dr. Rinaldi could say anything.

Gail Rinaldi hung up. Everything was falling apart. This wasn't the way it was supposed to be. She picked the phone back up and hit numbers.

"Hello," a voice drawled at the other end.

"This is Gail. We've got problems." The voice changed to all business. "What kind of problems?"

After Gail had explained the phone call she'd received, she waited for the response. The voice told her, "Mmm. Let me think a minute. OK, if she shows up there, I want you to get her in your car and bring her to the apartment. I'll take care of things from there."

"What does that mean?"

"Don't worry about it, sweetheart. It will be my problem after that."

"I don't want her to be hurt."

"Would you rather that she go to the media and tell them what you did to her?"

"I don't want that either, but . . ."

"Take your pick. You can protect her, or you can protect yourself. Which do you want me to do, darling?"

It was a stalemate. Nobody spoke. Finally Dr. Rinaldi broke the silence. "Fine, I'll get her to the apartment. What if she doesn't show up?"

"Then, you come to the apartment anyway. It's been way too long since we've seen each other. Just be sure to

Chapter Twenty-one

bring your cell phone and let your service know they should forward any calls from her to you immediately."

"Fine."

"Don't be upset. I'll take care of everything."

Chapter Twenty-two

Jenni took a deep breath. She didn't know what was going to happen but something would. She had no intentions of meeting with Dr. Rinaldi at her clinic, but she wanted to see what would happen when she didn't show up. Maybe Dr. Rinaldi's partner would show up and Jenni would finally know who killed Michael.

She drove the rented Escort slowly. She didn't want to get stopped for speeding, and she needed the time to calm herself. The clinic was in an exclusive lakefront community. There was no sign identifying it, but she recognized it immediately.

From the outside it looked like the other luxury homes in the neighborhood except that it had a small parking lot located in the back of the house. A part of Jenni wanted to drive into that lot and go confront Gail Rinaldi, but it wasn't the right time.

Shattered

Jenni couldn't just keep driving past the house without causing suspicion in such an exclusive neighborhood. To complicate matters, it was on a cul-de-sac. She drove to the end of the street and parked.

She sat watching cars. She didn't have much of a plan other than seeing what would happen when she didn't show up at the clinic. She looked at her watch. It had been twenty-five minutes since her call to Dr. Rinaldi. Forty-five minutes more crawled by before Jenni saw a car slowly pulling out of the drive and heading toward where she was parked.

Jenni watched Dr. Rinaldi drive past her. Jenni started the Escort and pulled into traffic. She didn't see the car that pulled out after her; she was too focused on watching Dr. Rinaldi's car.

Jenni followed Dr. Rinaldi to the university area. Jenni felt a stab of disappointment. No doubt she was teaching a class or doing research for the university, but Jenni was surprised when she pulled up in front of an old apartment buildings that had seen better days.

Surely, this was not where the great Dr. Rinaldi lived.

Gail Rinaldi hurried up to the apartment building's entrance. It had been more than three weeks since she'd seen her lover. There'd been excuse after excuse. She'd almost given up, assuming that the relationship was over now that her special services weren't needed anymore.

She could feel her heart speed up in anticipation as she opened the lock. The anticipation was short-lived.

Chapter Twenty-two

Her lover was pacing the perimeter of the room nervously. She looked at the other man in the room and suddenly felt queasy.

He nodded at the other person in the apartment and walked out of the apartment, not saying a word to anyone when he left. Gail turned to her lover.

"What's going on?"

"Nothing for you to concern yourself with, darling. You need to leave now."

"Why? I just got here. What's going on?"

"Don't ask any questions. Just leave by the back door. I will call you later."

"I'm not leaving until you tell me what's going on."

"You have to go before you get hurt." He grabbed her by the wrist and gave her a shove towards the door. "Just go."

Gail knew that she was faced with an important decision. She could leave and just pretend the night never happened, or she could take responsibility and try to stop whatever was about to happen. She'd thought she would be able to just let it happen, but she couldn't.

He gave her a shove toward the door and Gail allowed herself to be pushed closer and closer to the door. Her lover opened the door and kissed her cheek.

"I'll call you later."

Gail started to step through the door, but then she stopped. She knew she couldn't live with herself if she didn't try to stop whatever was about to happen. She'd always tried to live a moral life, but she seemed to have lost more and more of that morality lately. It had become easier and easier to look the other way, but not this time. She shut the door and turned back to face her lover. He gave her a disgusted look and walked out the door.

Jenni waited for a few minutes and then rushed into the apartment building. She looked at the mailboxes and saw GR on one for the third floor. She stepped inside and found the elevator. The door opened and she stepped in. Just as the elevator was about to close, in stepped another person. She looked up to smile, but the smile turned into a look of horror.

She was looking into the steel gray eyes of her attacker from the Bahamas. The scar was pink and ragged on his throat. For one absurd moment before the panic, she wondered how he got it. Her mouth moved but nothing came out.

"Nice to see you again, Jenni."

Hearing her name come out of his mouth shocked her back to reality. She glanced at the elevator light and saw they were about to stop. The elevator stopped and the door slid open. With all her strength, she propelled herself into him as the door open.

She was lucky. She surprised him, and he lost his balance and fell. She jumped over him, but he grabbed her ankle. With her other foot, she stepped on his hand. He yelled and let go.

Chapter Twenty-two

She turned and ran straight into the arms of Billy Bob.

"Oh, thank God, you're here. Get him. It's the man from the Bahamas. He must be part of it," she managed to gasp.

"It's OK. Don't worry about him. I'll take care of him in a minute. Let's get you in here where you'll be safe." He led her to an apartment door. He opened it and pushed her in the apartment.

Before Billy Bob could shut the door, she saw the man from the elevator standing behind Billy Bob with a big smirk on his face. Instant understanding dawned on her. She pushed at Billy Bob, but he was ready for her and simply pushed her harder. She toppled into the apartment. Her head came down and hit the edge of the coffee table hard.

She moaned in pain.

Billy Bob and the other man walked into the apartment after her.

She jumped up and screamed at him, "You're not FBI."

"Bingo! Give the woman a kewpie doll." Billy Bob spoke with an exaggerated southern accent. She attempted to push her way past both men. They each grabbed an arm, and before she knew what was happening, they had duct-taped her mouth and her arms. When they were finished, they tossed her to the floor like a sack of potatoes.

Her head throbbed.

Shattered

"Are you crazy? Let her go."

Jenni looked toward the voice. Gail Rinaldi was screaming at the two men. Her eyes were wide with terror. She looking horrified.

"What is she doing here? You were supposed to get rid of her," Billy Bob growled as he glared at his sister.

"I tried to make her leave but she wouldn't go. She just had to talk to you." Annie rolled her eyes in disgust. "All of a sudden, she's got morals."

There stood Annie Myers, but not with her mousy brown hair and her coke-bottle glasses. Instead, she had on skintight jeans tucked inside hiking boots and a skimpy halter-top. Her mousy brown hair had been brushed to a shine and had a sexy tousled look to it. Annie stood there looking calm and collected as she spoke to Billy Bob.

Jenni thought she must be dreaming or hallucinating. She must have passed out when she hit her head. Jenni looked back and forth from Billy Bob and Annie Myers and knew it wasn't a dream.

A gurgled sound came out from under her taped mouth. They all looked back at Jenni as if they had forgotten she was in the room. Gail Rinaldi ran toward Jenni, but both men grabbed her.

Gail was stronger than Jenni and gave them more of a battle, but in the end it didn't matter. Annie stood watching the two men struggle with Gail Rinaldi. She showed no sign of emotion as the men taped her arms

Chapter Twenty-two

and mouth just as they'd done to Jenni. Billy Bob looked over at Annie, his jaw muscles twitching in anger.

"Why didn't you get her out of here? Now we've got two of 'em to get rid of. You know the boss isn't going to be happy about it. He didn't want this to turn messy."

"No, the boss will be mad at you. Daddy never gets mad at me." Annie sauntered over to the couch where Gail Rinaldi had been tossed. "Why didn't you just leave like I asked you to? Now you've gone and gotten Billy Bob mad. There's no telling what he might do when he's mad."

Billy Bob walked over to Gail and grabbed her by the hair and pulled her face up to his own. His voice lowered to a whisper. "I did like you. Really, I did. We had a lot of fun together. We never had any plans to hurt you. Why couldn't you just do what you were told?"

Annie gave an exaggerated shrug. "Sorry, Gail." Then she looked at Jenni, and as an afterthought, said, "I really hoped you would just forget about all this, Jenni. I tried to keep you safe, but you just had to have it your way. It wasn't any of your concern. You didn't have to die. You should have left well enough alone. You have no one to blame but yourself. By the way, have you met my brother?"

She turned and looked at Billy Bob. "This will actually be better now that I think about it. Make it look like a murder suicide. Do what you have to do."

And with that she walked out of the apartment without a glance back at either woman.

Chapter Twenty-three

Even in the midst of her terror, Jenni marveled at the transformation of Annie Myers. She'd gone from being a nerd to a she-devil. It would never have occurred to Jenni that Annie was capable of such coldness and treachery. How could she have fooled people for so long with that sexless mousy act?

Michael had trusted her completely, and he had excellent instincts when it came to people. Jenni's stomach lurched when she realized that Annie Myers had murdered Michael. She had put pills in his morning coffee and then sat there and chatted with him as he drank it. She closed her eyes and forced the images away.

"What are we going to do now?" The voice of the man with steel gray eyes brought her back to reality quickly. Billy Bob stood in the middle of the room looking at the two women.

Shattered

He bared his teeth in a smile. "The doctor here did the renting of the apartment, and Annie made sure that she was never seen coming or going. We'll do it like Annie said. We make it look like Mrs. Hamilton followed the good doctor here and killed her after mistakenly deciding that the doctor was somehow responsible for her husband's death." He shook his head sadly. "Then of course, after Jenni shot the good doctor, she was filled with so much remorse that she decided to kill herself. How's that sound, Tonio?"

"Sounds good to me. Do we shoot 'em both?"

"No, I don't think so. Mrs. Hamilton here shot the doctor, but then she did herself in by turning on the gas. Unfortunately, there was a candle lit and the house exploded. Which will basically wipe out any usable forensic evidence."

His eyes never left Jenni while he described step by step how he would kill her. How could Jenni have thought he had kind eyes? She looked away and her eyes met Dr. Rinaldi's. She looked as terrified as Jenni felt. Jenni's head throbbed, and she wanted to sleep, but she knew that must be a concussion from hitting her head on the table.

Billy Bob went to the kitchen. He walked back into the room, wiping the gun down with a towel. *No fingerprints.* Jenni knew she had to do something. She looked around the room trying to figure out something to do.

Chapter Twenty-three

They had bound her arms and mouth but not her legs. Her legs were her only weapons.

She watched Tonio, who was watching Billy Bob wipe down the gun. She looked about her frantically trying to figure out what to do. Her eyes came to rest on the window. An idea formed.

The apartment was on the third floor, but she had no choice. It was the only way out. The fall might kill her but it might not. Either way, she couldn't just sit and watch them blow up the apartment building and all the people in it.

She took a deep breath. In one movement, she stood up and charged toward the window. She heard Billy Bob cursing at her just as she hurled herself at the window. She felt her shoulder momentarily stop as it met the window but then heard the crunch of glass and felt the window give way.

She pushed harder using her shoulder. She felt the jagged edge of glass as it sliced across her shoulder. A slight breeze caressed her face. She lifted her legs to finish the jump, but she felt arms encircle them. As he dragged her back in, she felt the shards of glass pierce her skin. She kicked at him and hurled her body at him. Both men worked to subdue her.

She saw movement from the corner of her eye as Gail Rinaldi jumped off the couch. She ran toward the back of the apartment. Jenni could only hope that Gail Rinaldi would be more successful.

Shattered

Jenni continued fighting, knowing that every second she used gave Gail Rinaldi more time. She saw Billy Bob's fist move up toward her. She bent low and with all her force knocked her head into his solar plexus. He grunted and took a few steps back, but she knew all she'd done was make him angry. His fist came back and hit her squarely in the face.

Jenni saw stars. Billy Bob pushed her to the floor. She heard a door slam at the back of the apartment. It was then that Tonio noticed that Gail wasn't on the sofa.

"Hey, the other one's gone."

They both looked stupidly around the room. "Well, go find her!" Billy Bob screamed in frustration. Billy Bob roughly grabbed Jenni's feet and taped them together. She got in a few good kicks as he did, but it didn't stop him.

Jenni heard sirens in the background. She held her breath hoping they were on their way to the apartment. The sirens were getting louder. Billy Bob looked up but then there was silence. Billy Bob gave a smile of satisfaction and looked at her.

"I guess it's just not your lucky day, sweetheart," he drawled.

A gunshot came from the back room. Jenni jerked at the sound. A second shot followed. Jenni shut her eyes and tried not to think about Gail Rinaldi.

Just then Tonio charged back into the room. "She got out. She was running down the stairs, but I shot her twice. She's dead."

Chapter Twenty-three

Billy Bob cursed. "Let's get out of here." He pointed at Jenni. "Shoot her."

Tonio lifted the gun and walked toward her.

Dear God, protect me if it be your will.

He aimed the gun at Jenni.

Please forgive me . . .

She heard the click of the trigger. Nothing happened.

"The gun jammed," Tonio whined at Billy Bob.

"Forget this. I'm leaving." Both men turned and jogged out of the apartment.

Jenni lay there, stunned to be alive. God had protected her.

"Thank you," she prayed over and over.

She knew she needed to get up so she could call for help, but she was so tired and her head hurt. She lay there not quite believing that it was over. She heard more gunshots and flinched. It wasn't over.

She struggled to her knees. The doorknob turned. Her heart beat faster. Was it Billy Bob coming back to finish the job? She tried to stand but the dizziness was too much, and this time she didn't fight it. She allowed the darkness in. She lost consciousness.

Chapter Twenty-four

Jenni woke up in the hospital. She panicked, but her mother was by her side instantly. Her mother was crying but managed to say, "It's OK, honey. You're fine, now. It's all over."

A woman in a blue uniform walked over to Jenni's bed. "Do you remember me?" she asked.

Jenni gave a small moan but still managed to smile. "Officer Lambert, right?" She was the officer that Jenni had talked to all those weeks ago about Michael's murder.

The policewoman smiled at Jenni. "That's right. Wanda Lambert. Everything's going to be fine."

A tall black man in a suit came up to the side of her bed. "Mrs. Hamilton, I want to introduce myself. I'm from the FBI. I'm William Gindlesburger."

She thought she was hearing things when she heard the name, the same as Billy Bob's. He saw the look of confusion on Jenni's face. He showed an ID. "I really

Shattered

am Special Agent William Gindlesburger, better known as Billy Bob. I know, I know. People think that Billy Bob must be some white southern boy but not this time. My father had a sense of humor." He gave a charming smile and she smiled back.

"That was the name he used. He said he was with the FBI."

"I know but he lied."

"He said he was with the FBI and that he was going to help me find out who killed Michael."

"How did he contact you?"

"He didn't. I found an e-mail account on Michael's laptop, and I sent a message. He showed up at my house. He actually broke into my house, but he convinced me that he was with the FBI, but that was after I met him when I was in the Bahamas."

"Well, he seemed to be doing a good job keeping track of you."

"I trusted him. How could I have been so stupid? Especially after he chased me in the Bahamas and then broke into my house."

"Because you needed to trust him. I'm only sorry that he intercepted the message that was meant for me."

"Didn't you get the message I sent?"

"I did get the message, but we decided you were just on a fishing expedition, and so we chose to ignore the message until we got the call from you yesterday. Then, we found out that there had been an explosion at

Chapter Twenty-four

your house. We obviously were wrong when we ignored the first message." He looked upset. "Very wrong."

Jenni didn't understand it all. She jerked up in her bed as the memories came back. "Someone needs to arrest Annie Myers. She killed Michael. I know she did, and she told them to kill me and Dr. Rinaldi. She was at the apartment, and then that man, Billy Bob, told her to leave. She did, but she seemed to be the one in charge."

"Just calm down. She's been arrested and is sitting in jail right now."

"She is? How did you know she was involved?"

"Gail Rinaldi told us."

"She's dead."

"No, she's not. She was shot twice but it didn't kill her. She told us the whole story, or at least what she knew about it."

"Was it true what Billy Bob said about Michael helping the FBI with the investigation?"

William Gindlesburger answered the question. "Yes, it was true. He certainly seemed to have good information."

"And you let them get away with killing my husband?"

"No, we just couldn't come forward until the investigation was complete."

"He said you had closed the investigation. That the FBI decided not to pursue it."

"The FBI never closes an investigation when we know people are running drugs. We had gotten someone hired into the company, and they were trying to find out who was running the drugs but the drug shipments had stopped after Michael's death."

Jenni shook her head; this was almost too much to handle. After all these weeks of trying to find out the truth about Michael, she finally knew the truth. She looked at the detective. "So, you knew the truth about Michael when I talked to you that day?"

Her brown curls bounced as she shook her head. She looked directly into Jenni's eyes.

"No, Mrs. Hamilton. I did not know, but you convinced me to do a little investigating on my own. I went back over your husband's papers, files, and appointment books. I started to notice a pattern of meeting someone named BB. Mr. Gindlesburger and I had worked together once before, and I knew that he often just used BB as his code name, so I called him."

It was so much. Tears ran down Jenni's face. The others were quiet as she sat there. "Where's Dr. Rinaldi?"

"She's here at the hospital. She's going to survive," Detective Lambert told her.

"Where's Tonio and Billy Bob or whoever he is?"

"They're dead," the real Billy Bob told her. He looked grim. "They shot at us and we had no choice but to return fire."

Jenni nodded and lay down. She couldn't believe it. Was it really over? Her mother put her arms around her. Jenni could feel her calmness slipping away from her.

Chapter Twenty-four

She tried to regain control but the sobbing started, and once the sobbing started Jenni couldn't stop.

She tried to tell her mother all that had happened, but she couldn't stop crying long enough. Beth finally told her not to worry about it, she would find out later. Jenni continued to cry until she fell asleep in her mother's arms.

Chapter Twenty-five

Jenni Hamilton looked in the mirror after putting on the black, pinstriped power suit that she'd bought for her day in court. Then, she made a face and took it off. She went back to the closet and chose something more to her liking, a soft, gray, cotton T-shirt dress that went to her ankles.

Much better. The gray made a perfect contrast to her hair, which she'd dyed back to the deep red. Her hair was longer now but still short. She wasn't sure why she was so worried about her looks, this day wasn't about her looks. It was about justice for Michael.

It had been almost six months since that horrible day in the apartment. That day was the beginning of bringing down a powerful crime organization that had been moving drugs into the country by using legitimate companies as a front. They picked companies that bought lots of raw materials from outside the country,

Shattered

such as the Marshall Corporation. Annie Myers would manage to get herself hired by the company. It was simple enough to add additional cargo in a few of the boxes without raising suspicions of the customs people. Once safely in the country and back at the factory, she would just work late and very calmly find the contraband and remove it without anyone being the wiser. The Marshall Corporation had been the fifth company they'd used in the same number of years.

Unfortunately, they hadn't known about Michael's compulsive need to check inventory. It had been on one of those inventory checks when Michael had found the drugs and contacted the FBI.

Jenni was proud of Michael. He'd known it could be dangerous, but out of a sense of responsibility, he'd helped anyway. Apparently, he'd asked Annie one too many questions. She'd drugged him that morning, and it was just by coincidence that it was on the same day of his arrest for the embezzlement.

Annie had embezzled the money from the company. It had been easy enough to steal Michael's signature stamp out of his secretary's desk and return it without anyone knowing that it had ever been gone. He'd never seen the papers that she'd stamped his name on. They'd just been lucky to find out about Jasmine DuPree and her son. Annie had intercepted a letter from Jasmine asking for some money as she snooped around his desk one evening. It had been the perfect set up.

Chapter Twenty-five

Annie had confessed all in a letter before she'd committed suicide while out on bond waiting for her own trial. Her father had disowned her after the botched business enterprise had made him a household name. He had been a powerful man in business and politics before the media had found out that his children had been involved in a drug-running scheme. The innuendo was enough to hurt him in politics, at least for a while. Annie had refused not only to incriminate him but also in the end had tried to clear his name.

Instead, she'd said it had been her and her brother that had been involved. She made it clear that her father had nothing to do with it. She apologized to her father for being such a big disappointment to him. The letter went on and on about what a great father he'd been and how he hadn't deserved to have his children become drug smugglers.

The FBI knew the father was involved but had no way to prove it. After the suicide letter, the media made a complete turnaround and now talked about the struggles of a man and his children, painting him as a victim.

Jenni was now in the business of rebuilding her own life with God's help. She'd never told anyone about the letter she'd received from Jasmine DuPree. She knew that Annie's father wanted revenge, and they would be the perfect targets.

Shattered

With the FBI's help, Jenni had made sure that Jasmine wouldn't lose her house or restaurant. Michael had left her more money than she would ever need, so she'd used some of it to help his son. One day Jenni would go and tell Michael's son about the wonderful man that his father was and the hero he had been.

Today was Dr. Gail Rinaldi's trial for her part in the episode. She'd ended up being the only one prosecuted for anything. She'd pled guilty and cooperated completely with the investigation. Jenni was going to court today to testify on behalf of Dr. Rinaldi. Gail Rinaldi had lost her medical license and that was punishment enough. Jenni had forgiven her. It's what Michael would have wanted her to do. It hadn't been easy but after much prayer, she'd done what she would have thought was impossible for her to do, but that was the day her own healing had begun.

It had been an awful six months for Jenni. She'd cried more tears than she would have thought possible but now each day her sadness became less a part of her. With God's help and her families and friends, Jenni had found her joy once more, and was beginning to think of the future with hope.

Jenni was thinking of opening a Christian bookstore with some of the insurance money. She'd always loved books and had even begun to think about writing her and Michael's story. It probably wouldn't ever get published, but it would make a great love story.

Chapter Twenty-five

Her eyes fell on the picture of Michael that she still kept at her bedside. She walked over, picked it up, and ran her fingers lovingly over his face. She set the picture back. She touched her wedding band that now hung around her neck. Someday, she would take it off completely but not yet. She ran her fingers along the letters engraved on it, "gmfl."

She smiled. Just like the geese, Michael and Jenni had mated for life. It had ended much differently than either of them could have ever imagined but Michael had kept his promise to her. He had loved her until death had parted them.

THE END

COMING SOON

A NEW MYSTERY
BY
LILLIAN K. DUNCAN

WELCOME TO

SILVER SPRINGS

WHERE NEIGHBORS

BECOME / KILL

FRIENDS

CHAPTER ONE

Matthew Travis put his hand on the door knob and inched the unlocked door open. The hairs on his neck tingled. His instincts were telling him that something was wrong and he trusted his instincts. His free hand moved to the gun at his side.

He unsnapped the holster and listened. There was no sound except for the ticking of an unseen clock inside the apartment. He nudged the door open a few more inches.

"Hello. Police. I'm coming inside," he called out. He waited. No response. He hadn't expected one. His heart was racing and he could feel sweat forming on the back of his neck. He called out one last time but there was only the ticking of the clock.

He thought of calling for backup but he didn't want to waste time waiting. Mrs. Stillwaters had called him only a few minutes before but she'd heard the screams coming from the apartment more than an hour before.

When Matthew had received the call, he'd figured that the noises had most likely come from stray cats in the alley but now he didn't think so.

He called out identifying himself as police once more but didn't wait for a response. He opened the door without calling for backup. Chances were that he wouldn't need backup even if the hair on his neck was tingling. In a town the size of Silver Hills, he rarely needed backup.

He walked through the doorway and looked around. From where he was standing, just inside the door, he could see the combination living room, kitchen, and dining room. His pulse quickened and he could feel his adrenaline begin to flow.

His instincts had been right. Something was wrong. The coffee table was lying on its side. The kitchen chairs were overturned and dishes had been knocked to the floor where they lay shattered. He stepped into the room and called out. Nothing. He walked back toward the hall.

Even though, he'd never been to this particular apartment before, he'd been to others in the complex more times than he cared to remember and since all the apartments had the same basic layout, he knew what to expect.

The Commons was an apartment complex that had started out as a retirement complex for low and moderate income people but it hadn't worked out that way. Instead, the Commons had become a magnet for people that either intentionally or unintentionally attracted trouble. He'd been to the Commons on countless domestic violence calls, several runaway reports, a few drug overdoses and not even a month before for a suicide.

Yes, Matthew Travis knew his way around the apartments in the Commons. He continued walking toward the hall but he did so with caution. His gun was pulled now. He wished now that he'd taken the time to call for backup earlier but he wasn't going to waste the time now. Someone might need help.

He came to the first door in the hallway. It wasn't quite closed. He could see rays of light streaming in from the window. He pushed the door open with his foot. The door opened easily and banged against the wall. The sound echoed through the apartment.

Sweat dripped down his neck and to his back. The air in the apartment was stagnant. It felt heavy and lifeless. He stepped into the room with his gun still pulled. That was when he saw it.

The blood.

There was blood smeared on the mirrors, on the walls, on the windows. The bed was neatly made but there was a large red patch in the middle of the white lace spread. Matthew's stomach lurched but he took a deep breath and kept moving.

There was no one in the room, just the blood. Now, he reached for the walkie talkie that was attached to his gun belt. He pressed the button. Yes, he would definitely need backup.

After calling the office for backup, he made his way to the room across the hall. The door was latched. He pulled out a handkerchief and opened the door. He didn't want to introduce more fingerprints to the scene. He stopped at the doorway. He blinked twice not wanting to believe what his eyes.

This was a little girl's bedroom. His eyes flicked to the doll house in the corner with several dolls arranged in front of it. The bed had a pink lacy canopy above it and there was blood everywhere. Under the pink lacy canopy were two people. A woman and child lay huddled together on the twin-sized bed. The woman had draped her body over the child's in a protective way.

Matthew Travis rushed to the bed. He touched the woman, cool to the touch. Still, he picked up her wrist and felt for a pulse. He didn't find one. He touched the child. They were both dead. He gagged and felt the bile rising.

He took several quick breaths forcing the bile down his throat. He was a professional. He could and would deal with this. When he was able to move, he went into the only remaining room in the apartment, the bathroom. The room was immaculate. The cleanliness of the room startled him. He'd expected to see blood. The room was empty.

His knees shook as he walked back to the living room. He had calls to make.

He hand was on the doorknob when he heard the sound . . .

Please visit me at:
lilliankduncan.com

To order additional copies of

Shattered

Have your credit card ready and call:

1-877-421-READ (7323)

Also available at:
www.amazon.com
and
www.barnesandnoble.com.

Printed in the United States
137970LV00001B/3/A